#1 ~~DAD~~ SUSPECT

"Those boots look like snakes," Carly observed.

Julianne put her hands on Carly's shoulders and marched her away from the door.

"Guy in the boots looks like one, too," I muttered.

"What's that, Deuce?" Billy asked, leaning forward.

"We're in the middle of dinner," I repeated. "What do you want?"

Billy hooked his thumbs in the belt loops of his pants. Which would've looked very Texan if he had been wearing jeans rather than a cheap, knockoff suit. And if the car out at the curb was a dusty pickup truck rather than a leased Lexus.

"Well, I didn't wanna go runnin' to the police without talking to you first," he said, raising a bleached eyebrow. "But maybe I should."

"Maybe you should."

The eyebrow settled. "When did you find out?"

"Find out what?"

"That I was representing Benny."

"I have no idea what you're talking about, and my pizza's getting cold."

"That I was representing Benny in a lawsuit." Billy Caldwell smiled, exposing his highly polished veneers. "Against you."

Stay at Home Dead

Jeffrey Allen

KENSINGTON PUBLISHING CORP.
http://www.kensingtonbooks.com

KENSINGTON BOOKS are published by

Kensington Publishing Corp.
119 West 40th Street
New York, NY 10018

All Kensington Titles, Imprints, and Distributed Lines are available at special quantity discounts for bulk purchases for sales promotions, premiums, fund-raising, and educational or institutional use.

Special book excerpts or customized printings can also be created to fit specific needs. For details, write or phone the office of the Kensington special sales manager: Kensington Publishing Corp., 119 West 40th Street, New York, NY 10018, attn: Special Sales Department, Phone: 1-800-221-2647.

ISBN-13: 978-0-7582-6689-7
ISBN-10: 0-7582-6689-8

First Mass Market Printing: January 2012

10 9 8 7 6 5 4 3 2 1

Printed in the United States of America

Stay at Home Dead

1

The dead man in the backseat of my minivan wore a T-shirt that read IT'S NOT A BEER BELLY. IT'S A FUEL TANK FOR A SEX MACHINE.

A bright red arrow pointed down below those words to the purported energy source of his purported sex machine. If I'd seen him alive before he ended up in my Honda Odyssey, next to Carly's car seat, I would've called him on it. Because the gut that protruded from the bottom of the shirt did, in fact, look like a belly made round and hard from years of imbibing.

But, at that moment, I was more concerned with the blood encircling the knife in his chest, why he was in my car in the parking lot of Cooper's Market, and keeping my three-year-old daughter from seeing his corpse. I regularly found flyers and business cards on the car windows, but finding a body inside was a completely new and disconcerting experience.

"Daddy, who's the man in my car?" Carly asked, leaning over in the shopping cart to get a better look through the window.

I wheeled the cart to the back of the minivan. "Uh, I'm not sure."

"What's he doing in there?"

"Sleeping, I think."

She looked at me with her mother's big brown eyes and narrowed them just like her mother did when she knew I was full of crap. "I don't think so."

I scanned the parking lot. The usual array of minivans, SUVs, and expensive German vehicles that traversed the streets of our little suburb north of Dallas. A sign as you enter town proclaims THERE ARE NO THORNS IN ROSE PETAL!

Would the dead guy be considered a thorn?

I looked at Carly while I fished for my cell phone in the pocket of my jeans. "Why don't you think so?"

She cocked one eyebrow at me. Jeez. When had her mother taught her that one?

"Because I don't hear him snoring, Daddy," she said confidently. "Like you. You snore. That's what Mama says."

Her mama, my wife, Julianne, did claim that I snored. I, never having heard myself make any sort of noise while asleep, denied the claim vehemently.

"Well, maybe he's just being quiet," I said, punching in 9-1-1 on the cell.

Carly thought about that and tried to duck her head again to get a look in the back of the van. I swung the cart away from the van and moved into the middle of the lot. The kid was apparently developing a taste for morbidity.

"Deuce?" a voice called behind us. "Deuce Winters? What are you doing?"

The voice, as it always did, caused me to wince.

I reluctantly turned around to see Darlene Andrews and her hair headed our way.

Darlene didn't just have big hair. She had monstrosity hair. Hair that could be skied upon. Hair that could be ascended. Hair that looked like waves off the North Shore. The giant blond configuration gave her head the look of a bobblehead doll as she sashayed in our direction.

"What are you doing, honey?" she asked, slinking up next to us, settling her hand on my arm and winking.

Darlene's greetings were always barbed with some sort of sexual innuendo. Maybe it was the way she swung her hips in the too-tight red pedal pushers. Or the way she thrust out her "not as large as she wanted them to be" breasts, seemingly ziplocked into a matching pink halter top. Or maybe it was the fact that ever since we'd gone to high school together, she'd been offering to take me to bed once a week.

I wasn't sure.

She reeked of Avon products and cigarette smoke. Her make-up appeared to have been layered on with a paint roller. Bright red lips. Thick purple arcs over her eyes. Brilliant pink circles over her cheeks.

I was wondering how much paint thinner she used every night to clean herself up when the 9-1-1 operator answered.

"Ah, I need to report a dead body," I said, trying to turn away from Darlene. Her two-inch-long nails dug into my flesh, though, and prevented me from getting too far.

"Excuse me, sir?" the operator asked.

"What's a dead buddy?" Carly asked.

I lifted Carly out of the cart and held her out to Darlene, raising my eyebrows and showing her a "Please help" expression. Darlene reluctantly retracted her claws from me and took Carly.

"A dead body," I repeated, attempting to step quickly out of earshot. "In my car. I'm in Rose Petal, in the parking lot of Cooper's Market."

Gum chewing in my ear. "In your car, sir?"

Darlene let out a shriek, and I turned just in time to see her raise a hand to her lips and step away from the van. Carly was leaning far out of her arms, still trying to get a closer look at who was occupying her backseat. Darlene's shriek, in addition to stirring the resting souls at every cemetery within a fifteen-mile radius, brought people running from the front of Cooper's.

"Can you just send the police, please?" I asked, shaking my head, wondering why I hadn't waited to do the grocery shopping until, say, never.

"On their way, sir," the operator responded.

I clicked off the phone and walked back to Darlene. I pried Carly out of her arms. Carly now shared Darlene's "I showered in catalog-ordered products and then went bar hopping" scent.

"Deuce!" Darlene said. "I can't believe this."

A crowd of about thirty was now standing behind her, gawking and trying to snag a look into the van. My totally uncool, but state-of-the-art minivan. Leather seats, climate-controlled interior, push button everything. Julianne called it a Porsche for stay-at-home dads. Pretty darn close.

"I know, Darlene," I said. "I know. I just called the police."

Darlene turned to me, the wide purple arcs above

her eyes arched like upside-down *U*s. "Why did you kill Benny?"

"Benny?" I asked, confused. "What are you talking about? Benny who? I didn't kill anybody, Darlene."

The crowd seemed to move their gaze collectively from the Honda to me.

She placed one hand on her hip and pointed her other hand at the car. "Benny Barnes." She pointed again for emphasis.

I hadn't heard Benny's name in a while. Maybe I hadn't wanted to hear it, but I couldn't recall the last time I heard someone say it out loud.

I handed Carly back to Darlene and stepped in closer to the van again, peering in through the side window.

He'd put on about sixty pounds since high school, mostly in that supposed fuel tank. His face was puffy and red; his neck ringed with fat. The athletic physique I remembered was gone, replaced by a Pillsbury Doughboy–like look. I hadn't looked much at his face when Carly and I arrived at the van. The knife in his chest and the blood around it as he sat slumped in one of the captain's chairs were a little too distracting.

But Darlene was right. It was Benny.

And I was screwed.

2

"Knee still bother you?" Sheriff Cedric Cobb asked.

"Not very much," I said.

We were standing at the edge of the parking lot, watching the police technicians meander around my Honda, staring at it like it was a science project gone wrong. Carly was sitting on the edge of the curb next to me, her chin in her hands, waiting for us to be told we could go home. And Darlene was off to the side, in a crowd, reporting what she'd seen in my minivan with a hand cupped to the side of her mouth in a failed attempt at secrecy.

Cedric, though his title as sheriff was more ceremonial than anything now that Rose Petal had incorporated and had its own police force, was one of the first people to arrive. Forced into desk duty, he sought out every opportunity to get out of the office and act like a cop again. He'd been one of my father's best friends for years, and I'd known him since I was a kid.

Cedric rubbed his square jaw and cut loose a low whistle. "I remember that hit Benny laid on you.

Sounded like someone snapping a pencil in half when his helmet hit your knee."

One of the problems with living in a small town, particularly a small town that reveres its sports, is that no one forgets a player or a play they did or did not make. Cedric himself was Rose Petal's unofficial high school sports historian. Benny Barnes and I had been tied by that small-minded legacy since that night during my senior year of high school when he ended my football playing days.

Cedric shook his head. "Woulda been nice to see you play at A&M."

Woulda been nice not to have had to pay for my college education, I thought. "Yep."

He shifted his weight, which at just under three hundred pounds was considerable, and squinted at me. "Bet that pissed you off, his turnin' your knee into spaghetti and all."

He was about as subtle as a stun gun. "Cedric, I haven't seen Benny in months, and I haven't said a word to him in years."

Cedric nodded slowly at that. "Sure. Just sayin', Deuce."

"Daddy, what are they doin' to my car?" Carly asked below me.

"They just have to check some things," I said, uncertain of what they were doing. "And they have to get the man out, too."

"Are they gonna wake him up?"

Cedric chuckled softly next to me.

"I'm not sure, honey."

Cedric squinted again in my direction. "How's it goin', not havin' a job and all?"

"I have a job, Cedric. I take care of my daughter."

He held up his huge hands like I was going to attack him. "Hey, don't take it the wrong way, Deuce. I'd love it if Emmy'd get her big old rear end off the sofa and get her own job so I could stay at home and do . . . whatever . . . all day."

The notion of a stay-at-home father was still a new idea in Rose Petal, Texas. When Carly was born, Julianne and I made a decision. She had a career that she loved and that paid her more than enough for us to live on. What I was making as a high school teacher and football coach was pocket change and would've flown out the door straight to day care. So I quit.

And most of the residents in Rose Petal still thought I'd been fired and that I had been sending out résumés with no luck for three years.

Truth was, I'd been a little nervous about it at first. I liked teaching and coaching, and I wasn't sure how I would do at home, all alone with a tiny little being that would depend on me completely. But I'd taken to it about a minute after we brought Carly home from the hospital, and I relished the reverse gender roles we'd created in our home.

Didn't mean I liked to take any crap about it, though.

"I have a job, Cedric," I said again, the familiar bristle of irritation tickling my stomach. "I take care of my daughter."

Cedric chuckled, nodding, his fat cheeks jiggling. "Sure, sure, Deuce. I got it." He paused. "Hey, I got up at five thirty this morning to get to work. What time you get outta bed? To go to *work?*"

"We get up at eight o'clock," Carly announced. "Every day."

We'd been talking about time recently. Apparently, she'd started to figure it out.

Cedric made a face, nodding like that seemed about right. "Eight o'clock. Boy, oh boy."

"Shut up, Cedric," I muttered.

"Uh-oh." He aimed his chin at a younger guy in a suit and dark glasses, inspecting the rear of the van. "You're gonna have fun with that boy."

"Who's he?"

"Willie Bell," Cedric said. "Detective Willie Bell. Serious as a hurricane, but dumber than a puddle of spit. That is unlucky that he pulled this one. Unlucky for you."

Detective Willie Bell stood a few feet behind my van. He removed his sunglasses, sweeping them off his face dramatically, then sticking the arm of the glasses into his mouth. He was speaking with one of the technicians, who pointed in our direction. Bell followed his direction and headed our way.

"Oh boy," Cedric said, grinning. "This'll be entertaining."

Bell stopped in front of us. A couple inches shorter than me at six feet, slim, a brush-top crew cut. His skin was pink, like he'd just finished shaving. Short, stubby nose and wide eyes shaped like eggs. His getup was right out of a cop show from the seventies. An orange polyester short-sleeve dress shirt paired with hideous gray polyester pants that were an inch too short at his feet, exposing white socks under black lace-ups.

He looked me up and down, the glasses still in his

mouth. Then he swept the glasses up and slid them onto his face.

Which I thought was sorta funny because the sun was behind him.

"You the owner of the vehicle?" he asked, his voice carrying the fake tone of a radio adman, deeper than his real voice, like he was about to offer me the deal of a lifetime on a used car.

"Yes," I said.

"Gonna need to ask you some questions," he said. "Tough ones."

"I'll try hard."

Bell raised a thick, furry eyebrow above the glasses. "Don't get smart with me, sir. This is a criminal investigation and a very serious matter."

"Sure. Sorry."

"Deuce is all right, Willie," Cedric said. "Just be cool."

Bell ignored him. "Tell me what happened."

I explained coming out of the store and finding Benny in the car.

"What were you doing shopping in the middle of the day?" Bell asked.

"We grocery shop every Tuesday morning."

"Ah. So you're unemployed?"

Cedric cleared his throat.

"I take care of my daughter," I said. "I stay home with her."

"Can't find a job?" Bell persisted. "Maybe you're a little angry about that?"

What I was angry about was having my morning filled with bozos.

"I'm not looking for a job," I said. I pointed down at Carly. "Taking care of my daughter is my job."

She smiled up at Willie Bell. “We get up at eight o’clock.”

Bell didn’t acknowledge her, which is exactly when I cemented my opinion of him. Tough to like a guy who doesn’t acknowledge a cute three-year-old.

“Hmm. Don’t know about that,” Bell said.

“Know about what?”

“Your denial of anger, sir. I hear you and the victim had some history,” Bell said, folding his arms across his chest and tilting his chin up. “Care to fill me in?”

I held out my hand to Carly. She reached up, grabbed it, and pulled herself up. I smiled at her.

Then I looked at Willie Bell. “Actually, no. Sounds like you already know what you need to know. So I think I’m done.” I looked at Cedric, who shrugged and waddled away.

Bell put his hands on his hips. “I’ll tell you when you’re done, mister.”

“No,” I said as Carly and I walked away from him to the other end of the parking lot. “You can tell my lawyer when we’re done.”

3

"So I'm gonna need a lawyer," I said.

"Good thing you married one, then," my wife, Julianne, said.

We were sitting at the kitchen table, about to dig into a pizza that had just arrived. Carly was in her booster seat, sipping from a bendy straw and stacking the half dozen thin strips of pizza I'd cut for her into a tower. Julianne had been home for fifteen minutes. Time enough for her to change into sweats and a T-shirt, to decompress from her job as a partner in a high-end Dallas law firm, and for me to explain our day, right up to the abrupt end of my conversation with Detective Bell.

"Guy was a total j-e-r-k," I said, slapping two pieces of pizza onto my plate.

Carly eyed me suspiciously. She'd picked up on the fact that when we spelled words in her presence, there was a reason for it.

"Did you just spell a bad word?" she asked.

"No."

"Then what was it you were spelling?"

I looked to Julianne. I blamed her for birthing an intelligent child.

"Your daddy just likes to spell, honey," she said, sliding into the chair across from me. "Makes him feel smart."

Carly nodded, as if, yes, she recognized my need to feel smart, then went back to building her leaning tower of pizza.

"And they impounded the van?" Julianne asked.

"Yes," I said. "I got Cedric to take us over to get the rental. Then I had to go and buy another car seat to get us home."

"When was the last time you saw Benny?" Julianne asked, picking up the glass of Shiner Light I'd poured for her. I say glass because if I ever even suggested that Julianne Winters might drink beer from a bottle, I would probably never be given the opportunity to sleep with her again. She's kinda weird that way.

"Don't even know."

"Guess."

I thought about it. I could remember plenty of times in high school seeing his ugly mug staring at me from the other side of the line. And I certainly recalled the night he turned my knee into Silly Putty. In a small town like Rose Petal, I saw him once in a while, but it was always in passing and we didn't speak. It was uncomfortable, and both of us hurried to be the first one to look away.

"Maybe about a month ago," I said. "Saw him coming out of Delilah's as I was driving by. But I haven't spoken to him since high school I'd bet."

"And remind me. Who'd he end up marrying again?" Julianne asked with an amused smile.

"You know who he married, Jules."

"No, my memory is failing me, Deuce." She sipped from the beer, her eyes wide. "Who?"

"Yeah, Daddy," Carly chimed in. "Who?"

"He married Shayna," I said, then bit off a chunk of pizza.

"Ah yes," Julianne said, as if it was coming back to her. "Shayna Linihan. Your first love."

"Stop."

"Shayna," Carly said, then looked at me. "Who's Shayna?"

I glanced at Julianne, shaking my head. My wife was beautiful, smart, and funny. Sandra Bullock with an attitude. Not much to complain about, really. But she did love to see me squirm, and she could poke the needle with the best of them.

"Shayna was someone I used to know," I said. I pointed to the tower of pizza. "Could you have at least a few bites?"

"Sure," Carly said. She grabbed the top piece, crumpled it in her mouth, and smiled. "Shayna was your friend. Right, Daddy?"

Julianne chuckled and raised her glass in my direction before taking a drink.

Shayna Linihan and I dated our junior and senior years of high school. Everyone thought we would get married. Hell, I thought we'd get married. But after I'd busted up my knee and my dreams of being a football star at Texas A&M went up in smoke, Shayna went up in smoke, too. Somewhere along the line she'd ended up with Benny. Though Julianne and I ended up together, I'd had the misfortune of not having any idea who she was in high school, a fact she still enjoyed bringing up.

All things considered, looking at the two women I now shared my life with, I'd gotten the better end of the deal and then some.

"Yes, kiddo, she was my friend," I said. "But I haven't seen her in a long time."

Carly nodded like she already knew that and returned her attention to her pizza.

"Don't worry," Julianne said, eyeing me over her glass. "It's a bunch of noise over nothing. You didn't kill him, and when they do the processing, they'll figure that out. It'll all go away."

I grunted. Julianne wasn't a criminal attorney. She handled complex civil stuff, and I trusted her opinion. But not much ever went away in Rose Petal.

Carly pointed toward our front window. "Someone's here!"

Visitors excited her like nothing else. Be it the mailman or the UPS guy or someone selling something, she treated each and every arrival at our front door like Santa Claus.

And she was right. A giant black Lexus was parked at the curb in front of the house and a man was exiting the vehicle.

Tan skin, frosted blond hair that was combed back and hung down to his shoulders, a matching goatee around his chin and mouth. His slate gray suit clashed with his alligator boots and bright pink tie.

"Hit me over the head," I said.

Julianne picked up her empty beer bottle, clutched it by the neck, ready to take a swing. "Wait. Why?"

"So I don't have to talk to Billy Caldwell."

4

The doorbell rang, and Carly scrambled from her booster seat to the door.

"Can we pretend we're not home?" I asked.

"Too late," Julianne said, following Carly to the door.

Carly grasped the knob, twisted with all her might, and swung it open.

Billy Caldwell cleared his throat. "Hello, little girl. Is your daddy home?"

"Yes," Carly said. "Why are you wearing funny boots?"

Suddenly, I felt much better about her opening the door.

"Carly," Julianne said, coming up behind her. She smiled. "Hello, Billy."

Billy ran a hand over his jacket. "Julianne. Good evening."

I moved into the doorway. It had been a few months since I'd had the displeasure of running into Rose Petal's worst lawyer. That wasn't an official title he'd won, just one that I'd privately bestowed upon him. His skin was a weird combination of orange and brown, the result of too much time in an overzealous tanning booth. "What do you want, Billy?"

"Evening, Deuce," Billy said, still looking at Julianne. "Hoping you had a moment."

"We're having dinner, Billy," I said. "What do you want?"

He moved his eyes from my wife to me. "Heard you had a little trouble over at Cooper's this afternoon."

"Did you?"

"Those boots look like snakes," Carly observed.

Julianne put her hands on Carly's shoulders and marched her away from the door.

"Guy in the boots looks like one, too," I muttered.

"What's that, Deuce?" Billy asked, leaning forward.

"We're in the middle of dinner," I repeated. "What do you want?"

Billy hooked his thumbs in the belt loops of his pants. Which would've looked very Texan if he had been wearing jeans rather than a cheap, knockoff suit. And if the car out at the curb was a dusty pickup truck rather than a leased Lexus.

"Well, I didn't wanna go runnin' to the police without talking to you first," he said, raising a bleached eyebrow. "But maybe I should."

"Maybe you should."

The eyebrow settled. "When did you find out?"

"Find out what?"

"That I was representing Benny."

"I have no idea what you're talking about, and my pizza's getting cold."

"That I was representing Benny in a lawsuit." Billy Caldwell smiled, exposing his highly polished veneers. "Against you."

5

When I was twelve and Billy Caldwell was thirteen, I punched him in the stomach. It was lunchtime at Ranger Middle School, and he was taunting a younger girl, maybe ten or eleven, about the large, chocolate-colored birthmark below her left eye. The mark looked a bit like a smashed brown crayon, but Billy wanted to know if a cat crapped on her face. Big, glistening tears rolled out of her eyes and over the birthmark as Billy laughed at his incredibly stupid joke. A couple of his buddies chuckled behind him, pointing at the girl.

She lived down the road from me. Saw her all the time, but didn't know her name. I did know, though, that if my mother found out I let anyone get bullied in my presence, I'd be crying from the belt she would take to my behind.

"Shut up, Billy," I said, stepping between him and the girl.

Billy carried himself with an unearned arrogance even at thirteen, and he lifted his chin in my direction. "You gonna make me?" Then he smiled. "She your girlfriend or something?" The smile grew. "Maybe it was your cat."

I was a year younger, but we were the same size, something that wouldn't be true for long, as I'd pass him the next year and keep on growing well over six feet by the end of high school, while he'd top out just under.

"Hey, Billy," I said. "Does it hurt?"

His smile got all screwed up. "Does what hurt?"

I stepped in and buried my fist in his gut. His eyes bulged and he bent over, his cheeks flooding with color. He fell to his knees and dry heaved.

"That. Does that hurt?" I asked.

He dry heaved again.

"Guess so."

School suspended me for a day, but my mother took me out for a hamburger to celebrate.

Now, twenty-plus years later, Billy was sitting on our sofa and I felt that same urge to knock the crap out of him. Some people just look like they could always use a good punch to the stomach, and Billy Caldwell was one of them.

Carly walked over to him, her hands behind her back, and smiled. "I'm three," she said.

I really needed to work on her people-judging skills.

Billy glanced at her, gave here an insincere, thin smile. "That's nice, darlin'."

"You gonna get to it, Billy?" Julianne asked from her perch in the doorway. "Because unlike the rest of the women in this town, I am not conditioned to offer you something to drink just because you're in our home."

Julianne's people-judging skills, however, needed no work.

He kept the fake smile on his face and looked at me. "You and Benny had a history."

"No, Benny and I used to play football against one another," I said. "Just like you and I used to play together on the same team. You played against him, too. That's not history. Those are facts."

Billy shifted his weight on the sofa, crossed one leg over the other, exposing more of the alligator boots. "You weren't the only one hurt in that collision, Deuce."

My knee throbbed for a moment. "Funny. I remember being the only one they had to carry off the field."

Benny hit me clean. I went across the field, caught the ball, and Benny nailed me coming from the opposite direction. He crashed into my knees and my left one caught, I heard a pop, and when I hit the ground, it felt like someone had set my leg on fire.

"I'm three," Carly said, holding up three fingers toward Billy. "And I'm almost four."

He gave her a tight smile and nodded, then looked at me. "He had shoulder and neck problems for years after that."

I shrugged. "Sorry to hear that."

"Your knee caused those problems."

Julianne burst out laughing, not bothering to hide her amusement. "So you're here to tell us that Benny was going to sue Deuce? For hurting his neck and shoulders?" She laughed again. "Seriously?"

I so totally loved my wife at that moment. She was my hero. Or heroine. Or someone I wanted very much to dress like Wonder Woman for just one night.

Billy gave a slow nod. "That's exactly what we were going to do, Julianne."

"Do you own a calendar?" I asked. "You do realize that was eighteen years ago and not, like, last weekend, right?"

His cheeks flushed. "He was hurting, and we had a doctor determine that those injuries were caused by you. Doctor was willing to testify."

"Doctor who?" I asked. "Seuss? Zhivago?"

"I'll be four very soon," Carly said, now holding four fingers up in the air.

Billy ignored her. "I'm not here to argue with you, Deuce. I'm here to be up front with you."

"Gee, thanks."

"Benny's dead, and just based on how y'all are reacting right now, I'd say I was right."

"About what?"

"About thinking I better tell the authorities that you may have had motive," Billy said.

I looked at Julianne. She was just shaking her head, like she couldn't believe we'd never moved out of Rose Petal.

"That suit, obviously, won't be able to move forward now that Benny's passed," Billy said, tugging at the collar of his shirt. "However, we are examining the possibility of a civil lawsuit."

"Civil lawsuit?" Julianne asked, sounding like she was about to giggle again.

Billy couldn't look her in the eye, so he looked just past her. "Wrongful death. Like O.J."

Finally. I finally had something in common with O. J. Simpson. Dream come true.

"I'll be four very soon," Carly repeated, holding

her fingers up as high as she could to get them in front of Billy's face.

Annoyance flashed across Billy's face. "Little girl, I am talking to your daddy. Stop interrupting."

Carly's face fell and her bottom lip jutted out. She turned and ran to Julianne, attaching herself to her mother's thigh.

"Get up," I said.

"Deuce, I'd like . . ."

I stood. "Get up now."

Billy pushed himself off the sofa.

I stepped in front of him, my back to my wife and daughter. "You ever talk to my daughter like that again, I will hit you in the mouth, Billy." I made sure my voice was low enough that Carly couldn't hear. "And even if you don't, I may just hit you, anyway, because it would make me happy. Take those ridiculous boots and get out of my house."

Billy hesitated for a moment, and I stepped in a little closer. He never got over me shooting by him in high school on the growth chart. Over the years, I'd come to realize that that was one of the reasons he hated me. There were plenty of others, but that was one of them. Silly, but true.

Billy cleared his throat, tried to smile, but it came off more like he'd swallowed a tack. "I'll let myself out."

I followed him to the door and watched him go down the walk to his car. He stepped in and drove away.

"What are you looking at?" Julianne asked after a moment.

I turned around. "Thought I saw a lizard in the bushes wave good-bye to his boots."

6

Carly, like always, quickly forgot about Billy's reprimand and after a bath and bedtime story was snoring before I left her room. I, of course, wouldn't ever forget it and knew I'd still be pissed off for days.

Julianne was downstairs in our room, wearing a Longhorns T-shirt and a pair of basketball shorts, working a piece of dental floss through her teeth.

She stopped for a second and pointed a finger at me. "Thought you were going to hit him."

I stripped off my T-shirt. "I *should've* hit him."

"Maybe. Blood would clash with the . . . everything, though."

I grunted and went into the bathroom, washed my face, pulled off my jeans, and fell into bed in my boxers. I grabbed the latest issue of *Sports Illustrated* off the nightstand and paged through it.

"Tough to read when you're using the pages as a fan," Julianne said, sliding into her side of the bed.

I grunted again.

"Speak, caveman."

I set the magazine down. "There are days that I despise living here."

Julianne smiled a perfectly flossed smile. "Wednesdays and Thursdays for me. Rest of the week I don't mind it."

"Come on, Jules."

"Sorry. Continue."

She was slipping into her attorney speak, but I let it slide. "It just gets old. The past never goes away, and that's all anybody ever cares about."

"Yeah, but that's part of the charm, too, isn't it?"

"I don't know that it is anymore, Jules."

She propped herself up with her elbow on her pillow. "You had a bad day, Deuce. But all of this is just silly. Billy can bluster all he wants about suing, but he's got a handful of nothing, okay?"

"I'm not worried about Billy," I said, fibbing just a bit. "I'm worried about Carly."

"Carly?"

I looked at my wife. "I'm not sure I want her growing up in a place like this. A place that won't ever let her move forward. Is that fair to her?"

Julianne placed a hand on my arm. "This is where we grew up. It's where we live. It's home. One bad day doesn't change that."

I shook my head. Truth was, I'd been thinking a lot lately about raising Carly in a small town where everyone would know her every move. There was no anonymity available to her. And like it or not, having Julianne and me as her parents wouldn't make it any easier. Her stay-at-home dad was still talked about as one of the best athletes Rose Petal had ever seen. And while her mother was one of the most successful people in town, she was also remembered as Rose Petal Queen of 1989.

Was it fair to impose our past on our daughter? Create absurd standards that had nothing to do with anything?

I wasn't sure.

Julianne leaned over and kissed me on the cheek. "Carly is going to be a wonderful person wherever she's raised. Her mother is beautiful and her father is . . . What are you again?"

I tried to look irritated, but it faded to a smile. "I'm cool and collected."

"Ah, yes."

"And stunningly handsome."

"I look forward to some day meeting her father, then." Her eyes flickered for a moment. "I am concerned about one thing, though."

"What?"

"Benny Barnes."

I nodded. I'd been thinking the same thing. Someone went to a lot of trouble to make sure Benny was found in the van. My van. And while I knew that I hadn't killed him nor had anything to do with his death, there was a knot in my stomach that didn't seem to want to go away.

"I know," I said. "Someone's not too happy with me."

"Well, yeah," she said. "But that's not what I meant."

"What did you mean?"

"I'm never sitting in that van again, regardless of when they decide to give it back to us." Julianne reached over and turned off her lamp. "So you'll need to get us a new van tomorrow."

7

Carly poked me in the forehead the next morning. "Get up, Daddy."

Julianne, per her normal routine, was up and out of the house early, leaving Carly and me to scramble our way through the morning.

I got Carly dressed and fed her a Pop-Tart while I jumped in the shower. She had a bright pink rubber band picked out for her hair when I got out, and after I tossed on a pair of jeans and a shirt, I managed to get her hair into something resembling a ponytail.

I feared ponytails when I quit my job. I had exactly zero experience with hairstyling before my daughter was born, and I was afraid I might end up taking her out of the house looking like a tiny Medusa. But with some patient teaching from Julianne and some minor whimpering from Carly, I got the hang of it and could now get her hair together without giving it much thought.

Which was similar to the whole stay-at-home parenting thing for me. I was terrified leaving my teaching job, being the one adult responsible for our tiny, fragile baby. I didn't grow up with younger siblings, didn't do any babysitting, and in general was uncomfortable in the presence of anyone wearing diapers. But after two days on my new job, I had forgotten about exams, homework, and term papers and was happily focusing on bottles, naps, and car seats.

And ponytails.

As I pulled the van into the parking lot of Rettler-Mott, Carly's preschool, I was, once again, grateful for the opportunity to stay at home and practice being a dad.

Carly jumped out of the van, and I immediately picked up the stares as we crossed the parking lot. Lots of eyes, lots of whispers. Apparently, just about everyone knew about the body in our van at Cooper's. Took less than twenty-four hours.

How very Rose Petal.

Carly grabbed my hand, her Dora backpack bouncing along on her back as we skipped down the stairs toward her classroom. She went to Rettler-Mott three times a week, in the mornings. It had been tough for me to turn her loose, but she was more than ready to be with kids her own age and start listening to other adults. I was finally starting to relax in the mornings and actually get things done rather than count the minutes until it was time to pick her up.

Her classroom was at the end of a long, narrow corridor, and her teacher, Sally Meadows, greeted us with a big smile. "Good morning, Miss Carly."

Carly returned the smile and charged past her into her room.

"Heard you all had a little incident yesterday?" Sally said as I signed Carly in on the clipboard.

"Yeah. Wasn't so good."

"I'm sure."

Sally was one of the few people in Rose Petal who probably wasn't prying for information with her statement. She had immediately taken me under her wing when I told her that I would be the parent she'd see most often with Carly. She liked the idea that I was breaking the mold, even if the other mothers still gave me the raised eyebrow. And she'd raised their eyebrows even further when she asked if I'd like to be Room Mom. We changed the title to Room Dad after I agreed.

So I knew Sally Meadows wasn't looking for dirt.

"Was Carly okay with it?" she asked, watching her dash to one of the art tables with several of the other children.

"Didn't seem fazed at all," I said. "Not sure she really knew what she was seeing, so I'm hoping it was no big deal."

Sally nodded. "If I pick up on anything, I'll let you know."

"I'd appreciate it."

Sally's eyes swerved from the room to over my shoulder. "Don't turn around, but someone's making a beeline for you. Try not to get stung."

I stepped back out of the doorway just in time to see Sharon Ann McCutcheon smiling brilliantly at me.

"Good mornin', Deuce," she said, with all the sincerity of a practiced politician. "Could you hang on for just a sec? Have something I want to discuss with you after I get little ole Austin signed in, all righty?"

Little ole Austin then proceeded to bite her on the wrist.

Sharon Ann's smile disappeared as she yelped

and yanked her hand away from Austin's jaws. Austin took off into the classroom. Sharon Ann took a step after him that clearly had the makings of an "I'm going to catch you and beat your little behind" walk, then caught herself.

The smile magically reappeared. "I'll be right back."

I slid over to the large window that looked into the classroom. The kids were busy occupying themselves with drawing and crayons. Sharon Ann was whispering something in Austin's ear, her teeth bared. He didn't seem scared.

Sharon Ann was attractive in a paid for kind of way. Expensively cut blond hair, expertly applied make-up, synthetic breasts behind a designer blouse. Her husband, Mitch, owned McCutcheon's Auto Mall, the largest car dealer in Rose Petal, and she liked everyone to know it by showing up in the newest vehicle to hit the lot each month. And while she had been friendly enough to me since the start of school, she was the one most irked by my designation as Room Dad. She served on the parent advisory board—the Women of Rettler-Mott School—and wasn't entirely sure that a father should be doing anything at the school other than writing the tuition check.

She emerged from the classroom and exhaled. "Deuce."

"Sharon Ann."

She placed a hand under my elbow and walked me away from the classroom, down the hallway. Deborah Wilbon popped out from somewhere and smiled at me as we approached.

"Hello, Deuce," she said.

Deborah was tall, with long black hair and a

pointy nose. Her daughter, Aubrey, was in the class with Carly and Austin. Deborah shared several things in common with Sharon Ann, including a seat on the advisory board and the same plastic surgeon. I had known Deborah much longer than Sharon Ann because she was Shayna's younger sister. Much like her sister, she pretended I was invisible after my playing days were over. Unlike her sister, who had married just Benny, Deborah was freshly divorced.

For the third time.

"What's going on, Deb?" I said.

Her smile brightened, like she'd plugged herself in, and she fell in step next to me as Sharon Ann continued to guide me.

"Where are we going?" I asked.

"Just outside," Sharon Ann said. "So we can chat for just a moment. Won't take but a minute, I promise."

I lifted my elbow. I refused to be escorted to our chat like they were mob hit women and I was about to be fitted for concrete boots. I opened the doors that led to the parking lot and let each of the women pass by. I momentarily thought about letting the door hit Deborah in the rear end, but I figured that was beneath even me.

Their smiles began to dissolve as the door closed behind me.

"Deuce, we heard about what happened at Cooper's," Sharon Ann said.

Deborah nodded vigorously.

I shrugged, offering up nothing.

"And we're concerned," Sharon Ann said.

"We're fine," I said, surprised at her concern. "Carly didn't really see anything and she's fine. So it's okay. But thanks."

The women exchanged a glance, and I realized I'd misconstrued their intentions.

"Yes, well, we are glad to hear that," Sharon Ann said, fiddling with the diamond bracelet on her wrist. "But we're wondering if a change might be in order."

"A change?"

Deb attempted a condescending smile, but it came off more like a sneer. "At your position."

"My position?" I looked around. "What? I should lie down or something?"

They both coughed out a couple of pity laughs that seemed to say "You have no idea how powerful we are, and we find your humor asinine."

"No, no," Sharon Ann said. "In your position as Room Dad."

I folded my arms across my chest. "Ladies, quit wasting my time and get to the point."

They exchanged another look.

"We just think it might be best if you stepped down from your position," Sharon Ann explained. "With everything that's going on, we think the class might be better served with someone else filling the position."

"Like one of you two?"

They both seemed surprised by the suggestion. Maybe they shared the same acting coach, too.

"It would just be temporary," Deborah said. "Until all of this . . . is handled. And it'll give you more time to look for a new job. You've been out of work for so long now."

Like that of a cornered dog, the hair on my neck bristled. "Taking care of Carly is my job. And there is no 'all of this,'" I said. "I'm not involved."

Sharon Ann raised an eyebrow. "Well, that's not what I've been told. There's going to be an investigation and . . ."

"No," I said.

Her perfectly lacquered lips stayed open. "No?"

"No," I repeated. I looked at Deborah, to ensure she understood. "No."

It was one thing to have to live by the pettiness and small-mindedness that pervaded some corners of Rose Petal, but it was an entirely different thing to give in to it. There was no way I was going to give up my oh-so-coveted position as Room Dad. I liked the job and I was good at it. I could deliver fruit punch, round up volunteers, and provide an extra hand in the classroom with the best of them.

"Not a chance, ladies," I said.

"But, Deuce . . . ," Deborah started.

"But nothing," I said, walking up the steps to the lot. "We're done."

"We'll call you, Deuce," Sharon Ann said.

And I would double-check that our caller ID was functioning properly in order to avoid that call.

8

The ironic part about leaving Sharon Ann McCutcheon at the preschool was that I was now heading straight for her husband. Fortunately for me, I liked him much better than I liked his wife.

Mitch McCutcheon graduated from Rose Petal High a year behind me but played varsity football from the moment he stepped on campus. Being six foot three as a ninth grader will do that for you, and he only got bigger, eventually topping out at a hulking six foot six. He was an unassuming guy, never using his status as a football star in Rose Petal for much more than a free pizza now and then.

He was an offensive lineman and parlayed his size and skill into a scholarship at Ole Miss. He came back to Rose Petal after graduation and immediately jumped into his family's car business, which he'd managed to grow into one of the bigger autoplexes in the DFW metro area.

RIDE WITH MITCH! billboards were all over town, and I had never bought a car from anyone else.

Two slick-looking, suited-up salesmen slithered

toward me as soon as I parked the van. I quickly repelled them by telling them I was there to see Mitch. The receptionist paged him, and a moment later, he lumbered out onto the showroom floor, a crooked smile beneath his crooked nose.

"Deuce," he said, offering a giant hand. "How the heck are you?"

"Been better, Mitch," I said, shaking his bear claw of a hand.

"How's Julianne?"

"Julianne will be much better once you sell me a new van."

He chuckled. "Wondered if we might be seeing you." He pointed outside. "Come on."

I followed him out the doors, past the two suits, who were now standing ramrod straight in Mitch's presence.

He didn't seem to notice them. "You've got the Honda Odyssey, right?"

"Yep."

"Like it?"

"It's a minivan, Mitch. It's not to like. It's to chauffeur."

"Gotcha." He rubbed his square chin, cut his gray eyes in my direction. "They really found Benny in it, huh?"

I nodded.

Mitch shook his head, and unlike most other folks, he looked truly sad about that. "Man, that is a shame. Sorry to hear it. I just sold Shayna a car two weeks ago."

"Oh yeah?"

"Yeah. Came down by herself and gave me an irritated look when I asked how Benny was doing."

He shrugged his large shoulders. “I left it alone. I knew they always ran kinda hot and cold. Everyone always said she still sorta had a thing for you.”

Blood rushed to my neck. “I hadn’t seen either of them in a while.”

Mitch’s eyes scanned the lot. “Sorry. Didn’t mean it like that. Just sayin’, you know?”

“I know.” I believed him. Mitch might’ve had less of an interest in the gossip of Rose Petal than I did. “Hey, any idea what Benny was doing these days? Work, I mean.”

“Managing a rug store over in Lewisville,” he said, a sad smile creasing his face. “Not exactly the greatest gig, I’d expect.”

Not exactly. It never failed to surprise me to hear what some of my classmates were doing with their lives. Some exceeded expectations, some were right where you’d pegged ’em, and others, like Benny, seemed to have taken a wrong turn and never found their way back.

“So. You wanna nother Odyssey, or you wanna try something new?”

“What’s new?”

“Lemme show you the Sienna. It’s a Toyota.” He shook his head. “U.S. still can’t figure out how to build a family car, but those little fellas in Japan got it figured out.”

After a quick test-drive and a call to Julianne, we agreed on a navy blue Sienna.

One of the perks of knowing the guy who owns the dealership is not having to spend four hours jerking around with negotiating and paperwork. Mitch told me what he could sell it for, I asked to have it for a thousand less, and he agreed. Which, of course, had me second-guessing myself, thinking I could have had it for two thousand less. Things like that let me retain a certain sense of masculinity in my daily life.

I was signing a couple of the few papers he did need me to sign right away when his cell phone chimed on his hip. He answered it.

And immediately his demeanor changed. Went from one of the most successful businessmen in Rose Petal to a chastised child right before my eyes. His entire body slumped in his chair, chagrin swept over his face, and he was nodding like someone was reminding him to chew with his mouth closed.

"Okay," he mumbled into the phone. "I will." He closed the phone.

"Bad news?" I asked.

"No," he said, shaking his head. "Just Sharon Ann."

"Ah."

"That didn't come out, right, did it?" he asked, but chuckling like he'd gotten it exactly right. "That woman sometimes."

Sometimes?

"Talked to her a few minutes before you got here," he said. "Said she saw you at the kids' school."

"Yep," I said, remaining neutral.

"I have no idea what the conversation was about, but I doubt I'd be remiss if I said I'm sorry for whatever she said," Mitch said, fumbling with some papers on his desk.

"No need, Mitch," I said. "It's nothing."

"Nothin' is rarely nothin' with Sharon Ann," he said, raising an eyebrow and letting his lips twist into a sour expression. "She means well. Just has a tough time pulling it off."

Mitch and Sharon Ann married right after they both graduated from Ole Miss. He brought her home to Rose Petal—she was from Biloxi—because that was where the work was for him. But most of the time, he seemed almost embarrassed that he brought her to Texas. It was easy to see why he would've fallen in love with her in college. She was attractive and looking to get married. She wanted to be a wife.

I just wasn't sure he knew what kind of wife she'd turn out to be. And that probably wasn't fair, because I didn't live with her every day. As far as I knew, she could've been completely different around him than she was around me.

But by the look on his face when that phone rang, I doubted it.

"She really starts giving you a hard time," he said, shoving the papers into a folder, "let me know."

I nodded but knew that I wouldn't. He seemed to have enough battles with her as it was. I wasn't going to get in the middle of Mitch's marriage.

Even if I thought he would've been better off marrying a skunk.

Mitch handed me the folder full of paperwork, asked to have it back the following day, and handed me the keys to my new Dad Van.

"Keep the bodies out of this one, huh?" he said, grinning.

He didn't have to say it twice.

9

Mitch knew the guy at the rental agency and told me he'd take care of getting the rental returned so I could take the new car. It was still too early to pick up Carly, and going home would just mean jumping right back in the car to go get her after a few minutes of doing nothing. I was contemplating how to waste the time when my cell rang.

The number came up as restricted on the readout. I answered it, hoping it was a telemarketer to mess with. "Hello?"

"Who is this?" a disjointed female voice asked.

"Who is this?"

She mumbled something that I couldn't understand. The voice wasn't disjointed. It was drunk.

"Who is this?" I repeated.

"How do you not know my voice, Deuce?"

"Deuce" came out as "Douche." "Because whoever you are, you're a little hard to understand."

"Jesus!" A deep, frustrated sigh. "It's Shayna, you dumb ass."

Wasn't expecting that. "Oh. Hi."

A ridiculous cackle ripped through the phone. "'Oh, hi'? That's all I get?"

I wasn't sure what I was supposed to say. She caught me off guard, and it had been a long time since we'd spoken.

"I'm sorry about Benny," I said finally.

The cackle burst into my ear again. "Benny, Schmenny, Wenny." She snorted. "I want to see you."

"Shayna, I'm not sure that's a great idea."

"Because you killed my husband?"

"I didn't kill Benny."

"Yeah, sure." She stifled a burp. "Don't worry. I'm not going to let you take advantage of me. Your precious little what's-her-name doesn't have to worry."

Well, that was good to know.

"Shayna, I don't—"

"Oh, just shut up and get over here," she said, running the words together. "My husband's dead. It's the do you can least."

"The what?"

"I don't know," she said, sounding like she might fall asleep. "I'm just sad and want to see an old friend. Is that so bad?"

I didn't have an answer for that.

She cleared her throat. "Plus, I have a crap load of vodka to share with you."

Who can resist vodka at midmorning?

10

Before I could smack myself in the back of the head, I pointed the new minivan in the direction of Shayna Barnes's house.

I hadn't seen her in months, but that didn't mean I didn't know where she lived. That was a common thing in Rose Petal. We didn't need the Internet or Google to find each other. Those of us that had been around long enough, word just got around. I couldn't think of anyone that didn't know that we lived in one of the newer subdivisions within Rose Petal. Likewise, it seemed as if I always just knew that Benny and Shayna lived out on the west end of town, right before Rose Petal gave way to the rolling farmland that checkered the landscape out toward Fort Worth.

And I was curious why she had called me. I was sure the vodka was part of it, but it was the rest of the motivation behind her call that was gnawing at my brain, knowing that it was her husband that had been found in my van. Coincidence?

No way.

The Barnes house sat on a corner lot at the entrance to their subdivision. The red brick the house was built from had faded to a dull pink, and the paint around the upstairs windows was peeling and cracked. The lawn was a mixture of brown grass and green thistle, dying of thirst. Weeds snuck out of the cracks in the driveway. The entire home appeared sad.

I turned off the engine and sat there, staring at the big oak front door. I had no business being there. I was there out of selfishness, to try and figure out what had happened to Benny so I could extricate myself from the entire situation. Shayna called me, but I was there for my own reasons.

And that was probably wrong.

I put my hand on the key, ready to turn the car back on and leave, when the front door opened and Shayna walked out.

Actually, she stumbled out.

Her long blond hair appeared dirty, unwashed, sticking out at odd angles. Mascara clung to the edges of her eyes, smeared and blotchy. She wore a wrinkled yellow blouse, untucked from the black, wrinkled slacks on her legs. One foot was bare; the other stuck in a black pump.

She stumbled out of the door and righted herself just before teetering off the front porch. She braced herself against the brick facade. "What do you want, buddy?"

I took my hand off the key, pulled it out of the ignition, and stepped out of the van.

I came around the front of the car and stood on the sidewalk. "Hey, Shayna."

She squinted at me, like I was standing in a fog. "Deuce?"

I nodded.

"Wow. Didn't think you'd actually come over." She stood up a little straighter, put her hands on her hips, looked past me, and smirked. "Nice minivan. Come with a diaper bag?"

"Haven't checked the trunk yet."

She squinted at me again, trying to see if I was serious. She was my age, thirty-six, but she looked about fifty.

"Benny's dead," she said.

"I know. I'm sorry."

She snorted. "Sure."

"I am, Shayna. I'm sorry."

She rolled her eyes. "Please. Benny was an ass." She lifted a hand off her hip, shot a thumb over her shoulder toward the house. "You wanna drink?"

"No. Thanks."

"Well, I do." She turned toward the house. "Guess I'll have yours, too."

I followed her inside and shut the door behind me. The house smelled like a bar, stale alcohol and cigarette smoke smothering me. The entryway opened up to an expansive living room, and Shayna plopped herself on a long leather sofa, the coffee table cluttered with a couple of vodka bottles, several glasses, and an ashtray.

She held up a half-empty bottle. "You sure?"

"I'm good."

"Excellent." She unscrewed the top. "Don't even have to use a glass, then." She held the bottle to her lips and took a healthy gulp. She swallowed, smiled, and set the bottle down. "Bet I look good, huh?"

She looked like someone had parked a boat on her for several days and she had just finally managed to crawl out from under it. In high school she took pride in looking better than every other girl in town. It wasn't an arrogant thing, but she knew how attractive she was and she took the job seriously. Long blond hair, a face carved in porcelain, features that had been drawn with a steady and exacting hand that was clearly a fan of the curvy women you'd find in comic books. Sexy emerald eyes. She was the one girl that caused all the boys at Rose Petal High to shake their head wistfully as she walked by, knowing that she wasn't just out of their league.

She owned their league and banned them from playing in it.

Unless, you know, you were a football star bound for supposed greatness.

"You look fine," I said.

She laughed much too hard and smacked her knee with her hand. "You always were funny, Deuce." Her laughter came to an abrupt halt, and she eyed me with suspicion. "Why'd you kill Benny?"

"I didn't, Shayna."

"They found him in the back of your station wagon."

"Minivan. I found him. I didn't kill him."

"Everyone says you did."

"Everyone is full of it."

"He was gonna sue you."

"I know."

"So is that why you killed him?"

"I didn't kill him, Shayna."

She shrugged and took another swig from the bottle, keeping her eyes on me. She set the bottle back down. "Our marriage sucked."

Uncomfortable was an understatement for how I felt at that moment.

"Shayna, look, I . . ."

"He got fired from his job," she said, ignoring me. "From the stupid rug store. Who gets fired from a rug store? Is that even possible?"

I figured her questions were rhetorical, so I kept quiet.

"Spending all his time on his big plans to get rich," she said with contempt. "Didn't do anything but get him fired and us poor." She grabbed the bottle by the neck and took a hard pull.

"When did he get fired?" I asked, more to get her mouth off the bottle than to make conversation.

She wiped her mouth with the back of her hand. "Two weeks ago. Got caught using the computer at the store for personal business. Working on his business plan."

"Business plan?"

She stared hard at me and folded her arms across her chest. "Why did you break up with me?"

"You broke up with me, Shayna. Believe it had something to do with me not being a football player anymore."

She ran a hand through her hair. "Oh. Right. Great move, Shayna. I'll bet *you* wouldna got fired from the rug store. Not Deuce Winters."

I wanted to tell her that I most likely never would've taken a job at a rug store, but it didn't seem appropriate.

"What business plan, Shayna?"

She stared at me like I was crazy. "What?"

"You said Benny was working on a business plan. That's why he got fired?"

"Yep." She licked her lips and made a sound like a balloon losing its air. "So stupid. All those kids running around in some big old gym. Shoot. Benny didn't even like kids. We didn't even have kids. But he was gonna dump all of our money into some freakin' rec center."

She was making no sense. "Shayna. What are you talking about?"

She polished off the bottle and dropped it on the sofa next to her. "Killer Kids."

11

"Excuse me?"

She rattled the windows with an enormous belch. "No. Excuse me." She giggled, then made an exaggerated attempt to sit up straight and smooth out her clothes. "Killer Kids."

"I'm not following."

She let out a big sigh, like I was the dumbest person she'd ever spoken to.

"Killer Kids," she annunciated very slowly. "A place for the little snots to play." She saw the confused look on my face and sighed again. "Jeez, Deuce. Don't you have a little kid to ride in that minivan? Okay. Do you know that place Tough Tykes? Over near the high school?"

I nodded. It was, in fact, all the rage. It was like one-stop shopping for children's activities. Gymnastics, swimming, martial arts, sports, parties. You name it, they offered it at Tough Tykes. We got the big, glossy mailer each month, giving the rundown on all the classes they were offering. It was all housed in a giant warehouse the size of a supermarket, and the classes were outrageously priced. Judging by their usually full parking lot, though, I was in the minority in my opinion on their prices.

"Benny wanted to build one just like it," Shayna said. "A competitor. He thought he could do it better and make us rich." She shook her head. "He and Odell had big plans."

"Odell?"

"Odell Barnabas. One of his partners in the whole stupid thing," she said, disgusted. "He used to work at the rug store, too."

"He doesn't work there anymore?"

"Hell, he got fired before Benny."

"For using the computer?"

"No." She waved a hand in the air. "And you wouldn't believe me if I told you why he got fired. Just believe me that Odell is a freaking moron."

Sounded like an ideal business partner.

"Anyway, Odell and Benny met a few times with Jimmy to find out how to run one of these places," Shayna said.

"Who's Jimmy?"

"Jimmy Z. Landry. He owns Tough Tykes."

That didn't jibe. "Why did they go talk to the guy who would be their competitor?"

Shayna's face screwed up in agitation. "I don't know, Deuce. If he wasn't dead, I'd ask him for you, all right?" She paused, seemed to reorganize her thoughts. "If you hadn't killed him."

There was no conviction in her voice when she said it. She was just trying to provoke me. I didn't want to make it worse. But it did irritate me just to hear her say that I killed him, as if the more people said it, the more people might believe it.

"Why'd you call me Shayna?" I asked. "Why did you want me to come over?"

"I wish you hadn't killed him," she repeated.

"Shayna. Why did you call me?"

"It was mean of you to kill my husband."

Between the alcohol and the grief, it was clear I wasn't going to get an answer from her.

"I need to go," I said.

She picked up the empty vodka bottle, spun it in her hands, and mumbled something I couldn't understand.

"What?" I said.

"I shouldn't have broken up with you," she said, her eyes filling up.

Eighteen years ago I felt the same way. She shouldn't have broken up with me. I was dumb and in love with her then. Couldn't see beyond her pretty face. She cut me loose three nights after the surgery, me standing on crutches in her driveway, she explaining that she just didn't have feelings for me anymore. Like the stitches in my knee somehow made me less attractive.

It had taken a while for me to get over it, but when I did, I laughed about it. The superficiality of our relationship, past tense, embarrassed me, and I was glad to be out of it. And then I finally met up with Julianne, because I'd been too stupid to notice her in high school and never thought about being with Shayna or any other woman ever again. I found the best, and once you find the best, you don't look back.

"I'm sorry about Benny," I said, heading for the door. "I really am."

She was sobbing now, but she pushed herself up

from the sofa and staggered around the table. "I know. Thank you." She looked at me through her tears. "I really wish you wouldn't have killed him, though."

I got out of Shayna's house before she could say anything else to me.

12

After spending the next hour cruising in my new ride all over town to get a feel for it and burn off my frustration over my visit to Shayna's, I went back to the school to pick up Carly. Despite the whispering and stares that emanated from Sharon Ann and Deborah and their little coven, I made it out alive.

Carly was less than thrilled with the new van.

"Where's my green van?" she asked as I strapped her into her car seat.

"The green van is gone. But now we have a new one. A blue one. You like blue, right?"

She looked around the interior. "Yes. But I really like green. Does Mommy know?"

"Mommy's the one who asked me to buy the new van."

She considered that, then nodded. "It's good to do what Mommy says."

And how.

I slid into the driver's seat, dropped the shifter into reverse, then slammed on the brake as a car came to a stop behind us, blocking our path. I waited for a moment, thinking they were stopping briefly, maybe letting someone cross the parking lot. But after nearly a minute, I turned the van off and got out.

Detective Willie Bell popped out of his Crown Victoria and pointed at me. “Stay right there.”

“What the hell are you doing?” I said, but staying where I was.

“Stay right there, Mr. Winters.”

Carly was trying to twist around in her seat to see what was going on.

Bell was wearing a starched, white short-sleeve dress shirt and a navy tie. Looked like a clip-on. His khaki slacks were split in half on each leg by a sharp-looking crease.

He yanked his mirrored sunglasses off and stuck his nose against the window of the van. “New car?”

“No, it’s a new plane.”

He shifted his eyes in my direction. “That supposed to be a joke?”

“Actually, yes.”

Carly waved from inside the van. I waved back.

Bell removed his nose from the window and stood up. “Why’d you buy a new car?”

“Because you have my other one.”

“We’ll give it back. Eventually.”

“Yeah, well, my wife doesn’t want it back.”

He slipped the sunglasses back on his face. “Why’s that?”

“Why do you think?” I asked, exasperated with his television show theatrics. “She’s not real keen on keeping a car we found a dead body in.”

His lips trembled in something resembling a chuckle. "Found. I like that."

I looked away from him because I feared my irritation with him would cause me to deck him, and no matter how stupid I found him, hitting a cop would not do me any good.

Unfortunately, moving my gaze from Bell to the growing number of mothers near the front of the school who were staring in our direction did nothing for me, either. Sharon Ann and Deborah stood in front of the group, shading their eyes with their hands against the sun, trying to get a good look.

"Heard you were out at the Barnes home this morning," Bell said.

"I was," I said, moving my eyes back to him.

"Trying to coërce Miz Barnes?"

"No. Telling her I was sorry about her husband. That's all."

"Right," he said, clearly indicating that he didn't believe me.

"Are you here to arrest me?" I asked.

"Just following up on things. Miz Barnes called us to let us know you stopped by."

I found that odd, but diving headfirst into a bottle of vodka at midmorning would cause you to do odd things. "Then she would've told you that I just came by—after *she* called *me*—to give her my condolences."

"She called you. Another good one." He smoothed the clip-on tie. "I'd suggest staying away from her for the time being. She didn't appreciate the visit."

I doubted she even remembered the visit, given how drunk she was, but I wasn't going to win an argument with Detective Bell.

"You aren't here to arrest me, then get out of my way," I said. "I'm leaving."

"We'll talk later," Bell said, backpedaling to his car. He caught his heel on the pavement and fell to the ground, smacking his head on the wheel of the Crown Vic.

I thought about offering him a hand up but decided I'd do a good deed elsewhere later in the day.

He scrambled to his hands and knees and jumped up. His sunglasses were askew, attached only to his left ear now, hanging across his nose. He attempted to straighten them, and one of the arms broke off. He threw the arm at the ground and stalked around the front of his car.

"I will see you later, Winters," he muttered.

"Have a nice trip," I said.

He froze and glared at me.

"Day, I mean," I said. "Have a nice day."

13

On school days, I usually dropped Carly off at my parents' house in the afternoon. With Julianne's parents having retired to Arizona, they were enjoying their role as her sole grandparents in town and Carly thought going to their place was a bit like going to Disneyland. I generally took those afternoons off to work out or to do the running around I couldn't do with Carly in tow.

My parents still lived in the house I grew up in, a sprawling ranch house on three acres on the north end of town, near the lake. My father had made lots of noise about getting out of town, going somewhere where they could retire and he could play golf year-round, but my mom just waved him off like an annoying fly. She'd been born in Rose Petal and she intended to die there, with or without my father.

They were sitting on the front porch, my mother with a novel and my dad with his head tilted back, napping. Carly began squealing as soon as she saw them. My mother reached over and smacked my dad in the stomach, and he jerked awake in his chair.

Carly unclicked her belt as soon as I turned off the van and leapt out the second I opened the door. She scrambled up the stairs.

"Grammy!" she yelled. "We got a new van! It's blue!"

My mother gathered her up and hugged her. "That is a very pretty van."

"Vans aren't pretty," my father grumbled.

"And there's no man in the back," Carly added.

"Well, we are glad about that," my mother said, grinning at me.

"That another Japanese car?" my father asked, squinting, even though his eyesight was better than mine.

Carly wiggled out of my mother's arms and shot inside the house.

"Doesn't Ford make a minivan?" my father asked.

"They do but it sucks," I said.

"Watch your mouth," my mother warned.

"Yeah," my dad said. "Chevys suck. Not Fords."

She swatted him in the ear. "Knock it off, Eldrick." She looked at me. "Had quite a day yesterday, we hear."

I rolled my eyes. "Does anyone not know?"

"Hard to keep a dead body quiet in this town," my father said, still staring at the Toyota. "Especially when it's a toad like Benny Barnes."

"You know anything about him trying to open a new business?" I asked.

For all the noise he made about leaving Rose Petal, my father was just as entrenched in the town as my mother. For twenty-five years, he had managed Rose Petal Regional Bank and had been one of the town's movers and shakers. Though he'd retired from the bank two years ago, he still held his seat on the town council, and rarely did anything go on in Rose Petal without his having gotten a whiff of it.

He shifted his weight in the chair. "The kids thing?"

"Grammy!" Carly yelled from inside the house.

"Don't give him horrific advice," my mother said to him as she crossed between us. She cut her eyes to me. "Like visiting an old girlfriend right after her husband died."

"*She* called *me,*" I said.

"Honestly, Deuce," she said, frowning. "Do more things like that and people will think you're dumber than your father." She disappeared into the house.

My father made a face at her.

"I saw that," she called back.

He shrugged and motioned for me to sit down in the rocker she'd vacated. "What'd you hear?"

I explained what Shayna had told me.

"Sounds about right," he said, nodding his head. "It hadn't gone very far. That guy Barnabas had made some inquiries about land and zoning but hadn't gone much further than that. Don't know what his finances looked like, but I would assume a retarded monkey at the zoo has better credit."

"What's Barnabas like? Shayna said he was fired from the rug store, too."

"Sounds about right." My dad took his index finger and spun it in a circle near his temple. "Nuttier than the retarded monkey. You ever seen him?"

"Nope."

He chuckled. "Well, I won't spoil that surprise for you. But trust me. If I was gonna go into business with anyone, Odell Barnabas would be in line right behind the last guy I'd want as a partner."

Carly's giggle wafted out from inside the house.

"What were you doing over at Shayna's?" my father asked.

"Being stupid, I guess."

"I'd say so. Thank God your taste in women improved once you got outta high school." He chuckled to himself. "Julianne will like that one."

"She won't care. You know that."

"Don't be upsetting my Julianne. Might disown you."

I was lucky. Julianne and my parents got along better than I did with my parents. I think they were shocked that someone who had so much going for her would choose to marry me. Not that I hadn't shared those same thoughts, but they liked to voice it every so often, more to goose me than anything else. But I think even they were still a little uneasy with Julianne being the breadwinner in the family while I took care of Carly. Not that they didn't approve. Just that they thought I might lose Carly at Target or something some afternoon. Which was always a possibility.

"Leave it all alone, son," my father said.

"What?"

"They found Benny in your car. So what?" He shook his head, frowned. "The bozos around here will try to make something of it, but the couple of right-thinking folks in Rose Petal will figure out. Shoot, I wish they'd give you more credit."

"How's that?"

"Some kid of mine knocks somebody off, I hope he's got the smarts to drop the body off somewhere other than the back of his rice-burning minivan."

I laughed. I never recalled my father being a funny guy when I was a kid. He was a little stern, a disciplinarian. Supportive, but tough. It wasn't until I'd finished at A&M that I started to get a taste of his humor.

"Stay out of it, Deuce," he said, tilting his head back, closing his eyes. "It'll sort itself out, and you can go back to sponging off your wife again."

Maybe he wasn't that funny.

14

Julianne loves lists. Grocery lists, to-do lists, Christmas lists, and Deuce lists.

When we laid out the ground rules for my staying home, we both agreed that leaving me a list of chores every morning would be a terrific way of driving me insane.

"I don't wanna see a list every day of things to do," I said. "I'll go crazy."

"I understand," she replied.

"I understand" was apparently code for "I don't care, and I am going to leave you a list of things to do every day for the rest of your natural life, and if you go crazy, our insurance covers mental health" in wife talk. I had trouble recalling a morning during the previous three years in which she did not leave me a short note, reminding me to go to the grocery store, gas up the car, call the doctor, or solve the Lindbergh kidnapping. When I complained, she said I was exaggerating, but that she would try and ease off.

She would then write that down on a sticky note

to remind me she would try to ease off and to pick up the dry cleaning.

Someday, I am positive, someone is going to sue 3M on the grounds that their little convenient invention led to relationship failure.

Amid the chaos at Cooper's the previous day, I'd left our groceries behind, and Julianne left me a note that morning, reminding me we still needed groceries. I didn't dare head back to the market, knowing that everyone there would be well aware of Benny having been found in the back of our car. Instead, I headed over to the Wal-Mart in Lewisville, where I knew I could get my shopping done in anonymity.

After filling the new van with the groceries, I sat at the light and the strip mall across the street caught my eye. Actually, it was one store in particular.

Land O' Rugs. Benny's former employer.

The smart thing to do would have been to take my father's advice and just let it all go. Take the green light, turn right, head home, and put the groceries away and pick up the house before my parents brought Carly home in time for dinner. And then make dinner, too.

As I went straight through the light and pulled into the parking lot in front of the rug store, I wondered if my father was wrong.

Maybe I was dumb enough to put a dead body in the back of my own minivan.

Land O' Rugs was sandwiched between a school supply store and a doughnut shop. The entire strip mall had the appearance of barely hanging on, as if a bulldozer could come by at any moment and wipe it from the face of the earth and no one would be the wiser. In all my years in Rose Petal, it was the first time I could ever recall noticing the occupants.

A distant doorbell chimed somewhere in the back of the store as I stepped through the door. A scrawny cat looked up at me from its perch on a pile of rugs. Short hair, orange and white striped, with one ear significantly shorter than the other, as if it had been clipped. The cat stood up, arched its back at me, and hissed.

"Boo," I said.

The cat scrambled off the rugs and sprinted for the open door at the back of the store.

I looked around. It was indeed a land of rugs. Piled in the middle, piled on the side, hung from huge racks that lined each wall, rugs were everywhere. The entire store smelled like new carpeting. An unoccupied desk and computer at the front were about the only things not rug related that I could see.

A college-aged kid ambled out from the back of the store, licking powdered sugar off his fingers. He reminded me of those young guys on reality TV shows—tall, well built, with bronze skin and a walk that indicated he was aware of his good looks. Short dark hair, strong cheekbones, and aquamarine eyes. He wore old jeans and a polo shirt that looked a size too small for him, like he'd just stepped out of the Abercrombie & Fitch catalog.

The cat trotted out behind him and retook its perch on the rugs, eyeing me suspiciously.

The guy finished cleaning his fingers. "Help you?"

"Manager around?"

"You're looking at him." He offered the licked hand. "Reggie Hamlin."

I kept my hands in my pockets. "You're the manager?"

He withdrew his unshook hand and shrugged. "Yup." His eyes scanned the interior of the store, looking for something. "Jake wasn't in here when you came in?"

"Jake? All I saw was the cat."

Reggie frowned, shook his head. "My supposed part-time employee. When he shows up, that is. Probably out chasing high school girls. Or moms at Wal-Mart. Dude can't get enough." He shrugged. "Anyway. You need a rug?"

"No. I just, ah, had a question for you."

The tiny flicker of optimism he'd shown when he thought I might be interested in buying a rug died, and he shrugged again.

"Benny Barnes used to work here?" I asked.

He nodded, nonplussed. "Yup. Until about two weeks ago."

"How come he left?"

"He didn't leave." A sly grin formed inside the tan cheekbones. "I fired him, man. That dude wasn't getting it done."

I glanced around the store. "Couldn't handle the heavy workload?"

The cat made a weird growling sound and hunched down like it was about to attack me.

Reggie laughed. "Exactly, right? How could you get fired from a place where all you have to do is, like, show up?"

I nodded.

"Look, my dad asks two things of me," Reggie said, holding up two fingers. "Show up on time and make sure we're all doing what we're supposed to be doing."

"Your dad?"

"He owns the store. I go to UNT, and he's making me earn my tuition." He smirked. "Teaching me lessons about life and things, I guess."

It wasn't a bad gig, really. Pretty sure he had plenty of time to get his studying done.

"But Benny was doing other stuff," Reggie said.

"Like?"

The cat stood up again and hissed. I resisted the urge to scare it a second time.

Reggie started to say something, then closed his mouth, oblivious to the cat. He ran his hand over his chin. "Hold up. Who are you?"

I was waiting for that question. "I knew Benny."

A confused look crossed his face. "Knew?"

"You didn't hear?"

Reggie shook his head, now taking genuine interest in our conversation.

"He's dead," I said.

Reggie's eyes went wide. "Shut up."

"Nope. Yesterday."

The cat hissed a little louder and stomped its feet. Almost terrifying.

The kid looked shaken and went back to rubbing the goatee. "Wow. Didn't expect that." He stopped moving and looked at me. "Wait. He didn't, like . . . kill himself? Man, come on. Over this job? No way. If . . ."

"No, no," I said, feeling guilty for even giving him that impression. "Nothing like that."

Relief swept through his face. "Good. I mean, not

good. But I'm just glad it wasn't getting fired that caused it."

I nodded and kept quiet. The cat stopped hissing and sat down, keeping a watchful eye on me.

Reggie thought about it for a moment, then glanced at me and remembered my question. "I caught him using our computers for other stuff."

"That's not allowed?"

Reggie shook his head. "No. Not even for me. I can't do school stuff or nothing, okay? My dad, he pays us to be here, and he expects us to work here. We don't get a lot of customers, but there's stuff to do. Vacuum, organize, paperwork. Work." He frowned. "I didn't wanna fire Benny, but if I hadn't and my dad found out, I woulda been fired. His store, his rules. At least when Jake shows up, he follows the rules."

"That's fair," I said, thinking he'd actually done a pretty mature thing. It would've been much easier to avoid the confrontation. "What was he doing on the computer?"

Reggie laughed, then stopped himself, as if he thought laughing was disrespectful to Benny. "He was trying to do this business thing. He wanted to build a school or something."

I didn't correct him. "I heard he was working with someone on that."

He made a derisive snort. "Yeah. With Odell. Now, that guy I was happy to fire. He was a jerk."

"He worked here, too?"

"Yeah, for about two months," Reggie said. "He was worthless."

"Why'd you fire him?"

"He tried to steal Bob."

"Bob?"

He pointed to the cat. "That's Bob."

"He tried to steal the cat?"

"Tried to put him under that stupid leather jacket he wears all the time and walk out with him." Reggie smiled at the cat. "But Bob fought back. Shredded his T-shirt and bloodied him pretty good. I heard Odell screaming and cussing, and I came out of the back. I still don't know why he did it." Reggie shook his head. "I seriously used to hate Bob. But I have new respect for him now."

I swore the cat sat up straighter.

"Thanks for your time, Reggie," I said, backing toward the door. "Appreciate it."

Reggie nodded and looked at me. "Hey. What exactly happened to Benny?"

I pushed opened the door. "Still trying to figure that out."

15

I took my groceries home and spent the next hour picking up the house. Between the previous day and that day, I'd spent very little time at home, and it showed. Carly's toys were spread throughout the house, the sink was filled with dishes, and the laundry was spilling out of the closets. I got things squared away and took some chicken out of the freezer to throw on the barbecue for dinner.

Not the most enjoyable stuff, but better than sitting in faculty meetings or Julianne's depositions.

I lay down on the sofa and dialed Julianne's office.

"Julianne Winters's office," a cheerful, female voice said.

"Hi, Melissa. It's Deuce."

The line buzzed for a moment. "Actually, this is Kathy."

By all accounts, Julianne is an excellent attorney. Professional, well thought of and, most importantly, almost always victorious. She is, however, quite possibly the world's worst boss. Overly demanding, forgetful and, as one former assistant described her, loony tunes. Her assistants rarely made it six months before slinking away. I wanted to have a turnstile delivered to her office, but I hadn't been able to find one on the Internet yet.

"Oh. Hi, Kathy," I said. "This is Julianne's husband."

"Oh, hello!" she said, mustering up the enthusiasm I heard from every one of Julianne's assistants when they were first starting out. "Ms. Winters was just telling me about you."

"Lies. She lies compulsively."

Awkward silence.

"Kathy, I'm kidding."

"Oh. Oh. Right," she said. I pictured her holding the phone away from her head and staring at it like it had just spit in her ear. "Let me see if she's available."

"Thanks."

It was just a guess on my part, but if she didn't get my lame humor, she would not be long for the job as Ms. Winters's assistant.

"Hey, babe," Julianne said.

"Hey. Breaking in a new one today?"

"She's been here for two days, and she's doing a nice job."

"So she's got what? Maybe just a couple more days left?"

"For someone who doesn't have a job, I'd expect you'd have more time to work on your stand-up routine," she said. "What's going on? How was your morning?"

"Fine. Quiet," I lied.

"Really? How did Shayna look?"

I sat down on the sofa again.

"Your mother called a while ago," she said, sounding pleased. "Spill it."

I ran down my visit to Shayna's and, just so I wouldn't feel guilty, told her about going to Land O' Rugs.

The line buzzed for a moment when I finished.

"Hold on," Julianne finally said.

I was getting the distinct impression I was busted.

"Had to shut my door," Julianne said when she came back on the line. "I didn't want anyone to hear me call you an idiot."

Yes. Definitely busted.

"I want you to think about a couple of things," she said, her tone measured. "They found Benny in our van yesterday. Automatically makes you a person of interest. Whatever. That's fine. But you're making it worse."

I felt the donkey ears sprouting out of my skull.

"But then you go see Shayna, the dead guy's widow—and, uh, your ex-girlfriend. . . ."

"That was twenty years ago, Jules."

"And then you show up at the guy's place of employment?" She cleared her throat. "I'm neither a detective nor a criminal defense attorney, but I don't need to be to see the guy they're going to peg as suspect number one. What exactly are you doing, Deuce?"

"Glad I didn't tell you about school," I mumbled, thinking of my confrontation with Sharon Ann.

"What happened there? Did you pull the fire alarm or something?"

"No, nothing. It's nothing." I sighed, properly chastised. "I'm just curious, Jules. And it seems like everyone is pointing the finger at me. But I didn't do anything."

"Exactly," she said. "So don't give them a reason

to point the finger. But running around, shoving your nose into Benny's life. How do you think that looks?"

The donkey ears grew out in full, and I felt a tail trying to force its way out of my rear end.

"All right," I said. "I'm done. Message sent. Back to my regularly scheduled programming."

She stayed quiet for a moment, and I knew she was trying to figure out if I was serious or not.

"Julianne," I said. "I'm done, okay? Just got a bit weirded out. That's all. I will consult with my attorney before making any more moves."

"That's better," she said, sounding appeased. "And don't think I'm going to let you skate on whatever happened at school today. I'll expect a full report when I get home. Behave yourself." She paused. "Hey, Deuce?"

"Yeah?"

"Sweetie, you ever go to your old girlfriend's again without telling me and I'll wreck your good knee."

16

My parents dropped Carly back at the house, Julianne came home from work, and we ate a quick dinner so we could go for a walk while the sun was still out. Carly strapped on her Strawberry Shortcake helmet and jumped on her Dora bike with training wheels, pedaling ahead of us as we strolled the neighborhood.

"So," Julianne said, squeezing my hand. "The WORMS are after you."

The WORMS. Women of Rettler-Mott School. They'd been too self-absorbed to recognize their own pathetic acronym when naming themselves. Unfortunately for them, Julianne spotted it immediately.

"Yes, the WORMS are after me," I said. "But I can handle them."

"I should hope so. Ladies in exercise clothes aren't that tough."

Carly stopped and turned around. "Come on, guys. You're slow."

"We'll catch up," I said.

She shrugged, stuck her feet back on her pedals, and got going again.

"You know you're doing a good job with her, right?" Julianne said.

"She's a good kid."

"I know, but you're a good dad. I'm amazed at all the things she's picking up," Julianne said, watching Carly pedal. "I know a lot of that is you."

"It's both of us."

"No, it's not," she said. "You're the one she spends the majority of her time with. It'd be easy for you to drop her in front of the TV every day, rather than get her outside, read to her, play with her. It makes a difference."

"I should probably try and negotiate a raise, then," I said.

Julianne snorted. "Getting to sleep with me is like getting a bonus every day. Consider yourself lucky."

I threw my arm around her. "Still. A little extra cash would be nice."

"Don't get a fat head. You still need some work on dressing her. And she enjoys burping far too much."

"What's wrong with the way I dress her?"

"Nothing, if her name was Carl."

"I dress her like a girl."

"Jeans and a T-shirt are unisex. Dresses are girly."

"She doesn't like dresses."

"She would if you'd put them on her once in a while."

"Well, it's not my fault."

"Why not?"

"You've never written 'Put her in a dress today' on a sticky note for me. How should I have known?"

I could tell by her expression that she wanted to

give me the finger, but there were too many children in the vicinity.

We circled the block a second time as the sun dipped a little lower in the sky. Carly was complaining about being sweaty and tired, so we told her this was the last time around. By the time we reached the house, I was carrying her and Julianne was pushing the bike.

"Who's that man?" Carly said, pointing to our home.

A guy in jeans and a long-sleeve oxford was standing at our front door. About my age, medium height, medium build. A military brush cut on top of his head.

"Help you?" I called out as we came to the bottom of the walk.

He turned around, surprised, then smiled. "Oh, I'm sorry. Didn't know y'all were out."

He came down the walk, and I braced myself for whatever he was selling. Oil changes, landscaping service, religion. We got them all in our neighborhood.

"You're Deuce, right?" he said, a look on his face that said he thought he was right, but not certain.

"That's right."

He produced an envelope and wedged it between Carly's body and my chest. "You've been served."

We all stood in silence, watching him walk away.

Finally, Julianne plucked the envelope from between Carly and me and opened it.

"Lemme guess," I said. "Billy letting me know I'm being sued?"

Julianne finished reading it, then shook her head. "No. It's a restraining order."

"A what?"

She read it again. "A restraining order. Filed by Shayna. Against you."

17

I got Carly in the bathtub while Julianne read over the restraining order.

"It's vague," she said, standing in the hallway, while I sat on the floor of the bathroom. "Doesn't really give a reason as to why she filed it."

"Doesn't it have to?" I asked.

"No. All that matters is she got a judge to sign off on one. You can't get within one hundred yards of her."

I leaned back into the wall, irritation and confusion settling into my bones. Maybe some fear, too. It made no sense. I wasn't sure Shayna was even able to remember my visit, much less take offense to it. And she called me to begin with. What could she be so upset at that she saw fit to bar me from having any contact with her?

"It doesn't matter," Julianne said, reading my expression. "You can't go near her to find out what's going on. We'll figure it out, but you cannot go near her. Hear me?"

"I haven't done anything wrong."

"I know that."

"But now I'm the bad guy."

"You're not a bad guy, Daddy," Carly said, her eyes peeking over the tub.

I smiled at her.

"Look, you aren't the bad guy, but if you wanna feel sorry for yourself and mope, be my guest," Julianne said. "The only thing I care about is making sure your butt stays at least a football field away from her. That should honestly be a rule in our house, anyway. We don't need a restraining order to abide by it. Understand?"

The water made a gurgling noise, and I looked into the tub. Carly was sliding around the empty tub like a fish out of water.

She looked up at me and smiled, her wet hair plastered to her forehead. "I let the water out."

"Yeah, you did. Let's get you dried off."

As I toweled her off, put her pajamas on, and brushed out her hair, I racked my brain for something I might've missed at Shayna's. And the only thing I could come up with was that someone was messing with me.

And I didn't like being messed with.

Carly hugged Julianne good night, and I took her into her bedroom. As I read her her story, I could hear Julianne's voice downstairs on the phone. When I finished the story, I put it back on the bookshelf and pulled the sheets up to Carly's chin.

"You're a good daddy," she said, grinning at me.

I kissed her on the forehead. "Thanks. You're a good kid."

She nodded, as if she'd heard that a million times. "I know."

I told her good night and turned off her light. I put away a few of her stray toys in the loft play area, made sure there were no monsters hiding in the two upstairs guest rooms, and headed downstairs to our room. Julianne was stretched out on the bed, the phone on her stomach, her eyes closed.

"Who were you talking to?" I said.

Her eyes opened slowly. "Hmmm?"

"You asleep?"

"Was." She rubbed her eyes and sat up. "Just exhausted."

I walked into the bathroom, feeling guilty. Not only was she working a job that required her full attention, but now I was forcing her to worry about me. If I needed a reason to back off of everything, I had it. But it was difficult to leave something alone that felt as if it had the power to upend my life.

I brushed my teeth and joined her on the bed. Her eyes were closed again, but they opened when I hit the bed.

"Who were you talking to?" I asked, taking the phone off her stomach.

She sat up again and sighed. "I called Sonya Luna. She's an attorney over in Fort Worth I know. She knows more about this stuff than I do. Told her what was going on with you."

The fact that she felt the need to call another attorney made the hair on my arms stand up. "You know I was kidding yesterday, when I said I needed an attorney, right?"

"Yesterday you hadn't been served with a restraining order." She yawned. "Anyway, I just wanted to touch base with her. In case we need her."

"Why would we need her?"

Julianne shook her head, irritated, and pushed herself off the bed and headed to the bathroom. "You know why, Deuce. I explained it to you earlier, and I'm too tired to do it again."

I lay in bed and stewed, alternating between anger and frustration. Anger because I really didn't think I had done anything wrong, frustration because I was causing my wife unnecessary headaches.

She emerged from the bathroom, face washed, teeth brushed, wearing her Longhorns shirt and shorts. She crawled under the covers and looked at me with sleepy eyes. "I didn't mean to snap at you."

I clasped my hands behind my head, staring at the ceiling. "You didn't snap. It's all right."

"I just wanted to check in with her and let her know what was going on." She yawned again and wiggled under the covers. "She's good. If we need her."

I had to admit that hearing that Julianne felt the need to call another attorney worried me. I think I had chalked up Benny's body, Billy's visit, Shayna's tears, and the rug store to just the usual goofiness that pulsed through Rose Petal. But I had missed entirely the seriousness of the situation and how I had made it worse. Dumb, dumb, dumb.

"Sorry, Jules," I said, still staring at the ceiling. "I've been a moron. I'll get my act together. I didn't mean for this to be something you had to worry about."

I waited for her response, but she didn't say anything.

I turned and looked at her.

She wasn't too worried, apparently.

She was snoring right in my face.

18

The next day, I did what any man accused of a crime he didn't commit would do.

I went to the park and played in the sand.

Carly didn't have school, and I didn't have anywhere I had to be. We spent the morning at the park down the street, Carly running wild on the slides and climbing walls and swings, me watching her out of one eye and catching up on some reading. She helped me clean the house in the afternoon, and then, after her nap, she assisted me in the kitchen, getting chicken tacos and a salad together for dinner, which we had on the table just as Julianne walked in the door. We had a pleasant dinner and did three laps around the block this time before calling it a night. Julianne was asleep by the time I came down from putting Carly to bed, and I crawled into bed next to her, smiling at our uneventful, normal Winters day.

The next day, however, wasn't so normal.

Sharon Ann and Deborah were waiting for me outside Carly's classroom. Sally Meadows gave me a look like she was sorry, but there wasn't anything she could do. I signed Carly in, gave her a kiss good-bye, and walked out into the hallway to face the powerful WORMS.

There were no fake or forced smiles this time. They were both serious, dressed in similar workout outfits. Black Lycra tights, Sharon Ann in a red tank top, Deborah in an aqua one. Serious, aerobics-doing women.

"Have you thought about headbands?" I asked. "Olivia Newton-John made them fashionable."

They looked at each other, confused, missing the irony of their outfits. As usual.

"Deuce," Sharon Ann said, getting right to it. "There is a special meeting tomorrow night. You'll need to be there."

"I'm busy," I said. "Stevie Wonder's coming over to show me his new hairdo."

"It's in your best interest to be there," Deborah added, ignoring me.

"What's the meeting about?"

They exchanged another glance, this one nervous, their confidence eroding.

"About you," Sharon Ann said.

"Me?"

"We've petitioned the school and parents advisory board to have you removed from your position as Room Dad," Sharon Ann said.

The anger cut through my gut. "You what?"

Sharon Ann held her ground. "Deuce. Don't take this personally."

"How should I take it?" I shut my eyes, gritted my teeth, and waved my hands. "Hold on. Back up. What is your reasoning behind this little male witch hunt?"

“We told you yesterday,” Sharon Ann said calmly. “With the cloud surrounding you, we feel it would be best if someone relieves you of your duties.”

“Temporarily, of course,” Deborah added flatly.

By temporarily I was pretty sure she meant permanently.

“There is no cloud,” I said.

They looked at each other and laughed, like I was one of the kids and I’d said something cute and silly.

“Deuce,” Sharon Ann said. “Really. We know what’s going on. Everyone does. First, Benny’s body . . .”

“Nothing is going on,” I said through clenched teeth.

“And now the whole stalker thing with Shayna,” she continued. “Really. We don’t think this is good for the kids.”

“Shayna called me and told me you showed up out of nowhere,” Deborah said in a disapproving voice. “My sister tells me everything.”

I was reaching my boiling point fast, and I needed to cool off. I was certain that screaming at them in the school hallway would not look too good.

“First off, I’m not stalking *anyone.* Get that through your thick, empty heads. And the kids are finger painting and putting glue in each other’s hair,” I said. “They have no idea what’s going on.”

“But, then, you do admit something is going on, correct?” Deborah said, smirking like she’d solved a riddle.

Sharon Ann nodded her approval. Like they were Batman and Robin. Or Dumb and Dumber.

I could hire a nanny. I could go back to teaching and coaching. Leave this freaking circus behind.

Wrong. There was no way I was going to let these

two fake-breasted exercise Nazis run me out of my daughter's preschool classroom. Not now, not ever.

"Don't come to the meeting, then," Sharon Ann said. "Might be easier for you to save face that way."

"I'll be there," I said. "You can count on it. No way I'm giving up my spot."

Deborah made a tsk-tsking sound and pursed her lips. "It could get ugly."

"Whatever," I said, backing away and heading toward the parking lot. "Oh. And you wanna know something else?"

They both straightened their posture as if they were being judged.

"You'd both be better suited to working out in loose-fitting clothing," I said, smiling. "Neither of you has the ass to wear tights."

19

The new minivan showcased its handling as I tore out of the school parking lot, irritated and on fire. I'd made last-second touchdown grabs. I'd faced down arrogant teenagers. I'd changed dirty diapers in public. There was absolutely zero chance I was going to let Sharon Ann and Deborah impeach me.

My stomach rumbled, and it wasn't just from the anger. I'd skipped breakfast, and my little confrontation had apparently spurred my appetite. So I headed toward Rose Petal Square.

Rose Petal Square was actually a street. The original downtown area hadn't actually formed a square or rectangular area, but the powers that be had wanted a town square that would draw locals and lost tourists. So they'd come up with the brilliant idea of naming a street Rose Petal Square in hopes of confusing everyone.

And it worked.

Right in the middle of the six-block length of Rose Petal Square was Delilah's, a diner that also served as the unofficial town hall. You wanted to get the proverbial pulse of Rose Petal, you had a little breakfast and eavesdropped at Delilah's.

It was also where my father, official town council member, had breakfast every day.

I found him at a back table with Cedric Cobb and Sheldon Monaghan.

He raised his eyes as I approached. "Well, well. If it isn't my son, the stalker."

I grabbed the empty chair next to him. "I will stab you in the eye with that spoon on the table if you keep it up."

Cedric chuckled and Sheldon laughed into his mug of coffee.

"Hear you got a little get-together tomorrow night, too," Cedric said, pointing at me with a forkful of egg.

"Jesus. How do you already know that?"

All three men just shrugged.

"What's all this business with Shayna?" my father asked.

"There is no business with Shayna," I said sharply. "It's garbage."

"Restraining order ain't garbage, Deuce," Sheldon said, then took a sip from his coffee.

Sheldon Monaghan was my father's oldest friend. They'd played ball together at Rose Petal back in their day, and they'd remained close ever since. Sheldon had parlayed his role as the town's most prominent Realtor into an eleven-year stint as Rose Petal's mayor. With his shock of white hair and ever-present bifocals, he looked about ten years older than my father. He compensated for that by dating women half his age.

"No idea why she filed it," I told them. "She

called me and asked me to come over. Nothing happened at her house."

"I'll give Gerald a call," Cedric said. "See if he'll spill anything."

Gerald Kantner was the judge in Rose Petal. Normally, he occupied the chair I was sitting in.

"I'd appreciate that," I said.

The waitress came, and I ordered pancakes, bacon, and orange juice.

"What'd Julianne say?" my dad asked.

"About what you'd expect. Told me to stop doing stupid things."

"Smart girl, that Julianne," my father said. "Excepting, of course, her choice in husbands."

The other two men nodded.

"Your dad was asking me about this thing old Benny was involved in," Sheldon said, adjusting his bifocals.

"Know anything?"

"I know Odell Barnabas is about as dumb as a dead fish," he said with a frown. "That boy is several crayons short of a full box."

We all laughed.

"He was trying to buy a couple of acres out near the lake," the mayor said, resting his elbows on the table. "Problem was, he didn't have any money." He grinned. "Wanted to know if he could finance without a down payment. He said he was working on finding investors."

"Did he have any clue what he was doing?" I asked. "Did he even have a plan drawn up? A design of the building? Anything?"

"My guess would be that he had it all drawn up on a couple of cocktail napkins."

"Let me ask you guys something," I said, looking at each of them. "Benny ever strike you guys as being dumb enough to get dragged into something like this?"

"Not really," Cedric said, speaking for his friends. "But Benny, he didn't exactly have it easy since that night he hit you." He shifted his weight in his chair. "He didn't handle it as well as you did."

My food arrived, and I dug into the pancakes. I wasn't aware that I'd handled the end of my football career all that well. I'd sat around and moped for six months, nearly flunked out of A&M at the end of my first year, and put on about twenty pounds, most of it from beer. It was only after I met Julianne that I got my act together and stopped feeling sorry for myself. And, to be totally honest, there were days when I saw kids going to practice or I caught a game on TV that I still had a twinge of self-pity.

"But if he gave this fella Barnabas any of his money," Cedric said, shaking his head, "well, that woulda been an all-time low for even Benny."

"Not your problem, son," my father reminded me. "Now, those tough women at Rettler-Mott? They are definitely your problem."

The three of them laughed loudly, and I stifled a smile by shoving more pancakes in my mouth.

They moved on to other topics. I loved hearing them talk. I always had. The ease of their friendship was evident in their words; the way they needled each other—and every other resident of Rose Petal—was born of sheer affection. There were much worse ways to age other than to sit around yakking with good friends.

Sheldon sat up a little straighter as I was polishing off my bacon. He adjusted his glasses. "You wanna have a chat with Odell Barnabas?"

I remembered Julianne's advice. "No, I guess not. Don't see the point, really."

Cedric started to laugh and looked down at the table.

The mayor jutted out his bottom lip. "Well, Deuce, you may not have a choice. Because he just walked in and he's heading our way."

20

The first thing I noticed about Odell Barnabas was his hair.

The thick black hair was greased and combed up into a massive, oily pompadour that protruded off his forehead, making him look a bit like a rooster. Thick sideburns crept down his cheeks, beneath his ears, and almost to his jawline.

His eyes were wide set and bright blue, so blue I was certain that he was wearing contacts. His nose was flat and crooked. I tried to locate his neck but failed to find it, his oblong-shaped head sitting squarely on his rounded shoulders. Maybe six feet tall, minus the hair.

He wore a black leather jacket, a stark white T-shirt that showcased a nice little paunch above his belt, and blue jeans rolled over the top of black boots. A cigarette was tucked behind his left ear, and he walked with his chest out and a bounce in his step.

But there was something about the hair that just creeped me out.

He nodded at my father and his two friends, then

looked at me. "I'm Odell. Hear you been askin' about me."

It was part Fonzie, part Vinnie Barbarino, part "I saw a guy in a movie talk like this once."

"Uh," I said, unsure how to answer. "I guess."

He lifted his chin. "You want in?"

"In?"

"On the thing."

My father and his friends were all squirming in their chairs, doing their best to keep from laughing.

"The thing?"

"I got it outside," he said. "Come on out. I'll show ya." He turned back toward the front of the restaurant, like he was checking to see if something was out there, then looked back at me.

And that was when I figured out the hair.

When he turned, the hair sort of wobbled on his head, didn't really move in sync with the rest of his body, like there was a brief delay.

The great big pompadour was a great big toupee.

And now I was having difficulty taking my eyes off it.

He pulled a comb from the back pocket of his jeans and ran it front to back through the side of his hair. I found it to be a gutsy move, because unless the rug was rubber cemented to his head, there was a fifty-fifty chance it was coming off with a single pull of the comb.

"I got it out in my truck," he said, now pulling the comb through the other side.

Why would you risk combing a toupee? Wasn't that what all the grease or mousse or whatever it was in his hair was for? Don't you style it before you leave the house and then put up a force field around it? Or, better yet, don't you order it that way from wherever you get them? Toupees-Mart?

My father's elbow found my ribs, and I managed to look away from the hair. "Uh, sure. I guess. Remind me, though. What exactly are you showing me?"

He shoved the comb back in his pocket and tugged on the lapels of the leather jacket. "You'll see, Ace. Follow me."

He turned on his boot heel and strutted to the front door.

I looked at the other three men at the table. "He doesn't bite, does he?"

My father shook his head and glanced over his shoulder. "Odell, no. But that hair very well might have teeth in there somewhere."

Teeth. Maybe that was how it stayed on.

21

Odell's truck was a station wagon, a hideous-looking brown and tan thing, complete with faux wood paneling on the sides, circa *The Brady Bunch* era.

He took me around to the back and busted out the comb again, running it carefully through the hair. "So. How'd ya hear about this?"

"Odell, I have to be honest with you," I said. "I'm still not sure what we're talking about here."

He placed the comb in his back pocket and checked his reflection in the dirty back window of the station wagon. "Killer Kids, man." He nodded approvingly at his reflection, then turned to me. "Gonna be huge, Ace."

Killer Kids. Of course.

Odell pulled the latch on the back door of the station wagon and rooted around in the interior. Piles of clothes, empty boxes, paper bags, and soda cups flew around as he searched for whatever was beneath.

Finally, he extracted a long yellow tube several inches in diameter and slammed the tailgate shut.

He walked around to the front of the wagon, and I followed.

He removed the leather jacket, tossed it high on the hood, exposing rounded shoulders and forearms that were nearly as white as the T-shirt.

"It's gonna be beautiful, man," he said, chuckling as he popped the top on the tube and a roll of papers slid out. "I'm telling you."

"I'll bet."

"Me and Benny, we worked our tails off on this," he said, unrolling the paper across the hood of the wagon. "Shame he's gonna miss it all."

I expected blueprints but got what looked like something Carly might be capable of concocting. Crudely drawn buildings in colored pencil were strewn across a long piece of butcher paper. Little cartoonish-looking people were drawn as if walking into the biggest square building on the drawing. A big flag above that building proclaimed KILLER KIDS!

My first thought: would the exclamation point actually be part of the name?

"This here's the main building," Odell said, pointing to the big building with the flag. "It's gonna have a couple of gyms, a swimming pool, some party rooms, and some other stuff I'm not sure of yet. Maybe some martial arts type of room, where the little suckers can karate chop wood or bust cement with their heads. I don't know yet."

His finger slid to a smaller square adjacent to the big one. "This is the weight room." His finger slid again, this time to a rectangle colored in blue with a little boat drawn in it. "Outdoor pool here." He grinned at me. "Kids can swim inside or outside."

"Sure." I pointed to a big orange circle next to the outdoor pool. "What's that?"

"My office," he said. "Thought it'd be cool to build it in a circle."

I wasn't sure what to say to that.

His finger moved back across the page to the opposite side of the main building, to a red and black bull's-eye. "This here, though, is what's gonna make Killer Kids different."

"What is it?"

He folded his arms across his chest, the paunch beneath the T-shirt pushing out a little farther. "The weapons area."

"Excuse me?"

"Weapons, Ace," he said, craning his neck at me. "We're gonna teach them little buggers how to shoot."

I glanced at the bull's-eye. "To shoot? Guns?"

"Lotta folks own guns around here," he said confidently. "Huntin', protectin' themselves, shootin' squirrels, whatever. The way I figure, kids better learn how to use those guns and we can teach 'em."

I scanned the street.

I checked the cars parked next to Odell's.

I looked behind me.

I was absolutely certain someone was playing a joke on me, but I could find no evidence of cameras in the vicinity, looking to capture my reaction.

I looked at Odell. He smiled back at me, arms still folded across his chest, fake pompadour standing tall.

Odell Barnabas was completely serious.

"You're going to have a shooting range at a kids' play facility?" I asked.

"Not a play facility, Ace. I'm callin' it a recreation complex."

"You think parents are going to be okay with this?"

He nodded. "Sure. We're providin' a necessary service for the little buggers." He grinned. "Don't want anyone shootin' an eye out." The grin faded into a solemn expression. "I figure we'll offer a week's worth of shootin' lessons to generate membership." He tapped his skull with his index finger. "Can't forget the business side of things, Ace."

I was trying to picture elementary school kids walking around with goggles, earplugs, and sweeping up their spent brass.

"Don't you think there might some insurance issues?" I asked, trying to be diplomatic. Explaining that guns and kids and Odell weren't going to mix obviously wasn't going to fly.

He looked at me like I was crazy. "Insurance? Ace, my truck here's covered and I rent my house. Not sure what insurance has to do with anything."

Oh. My.

"I can get you in for as little as ten thousand," Odell said, leaning against the wagon. "I've got several silent investors, fellas who just want me to turn their money into more money. Of course, you could buy in with more. Bigger buy in, bigger return."

I needed to change the direction of the conversation before Santa Claus drove by with the Easter Bunny.

"How much did Benny buy in with?" I asked.

He rolled his shoulders a couple of times and fiddled with the cigarette behind his ear. "Thirty. He was workin' on another twenty."

"Thirty thousand?"

"Yep. He was all in, Ace." He shook his head, and his expression soured for the first time. "Not like his wife."

"Shayna didn't like the idea?"

He pulled the cigarette off his ear and rolled it around between his fingers. "Shayna. Things got kinda messed up with her, Ace."

"How's that?"

He shoved the cigarette in the corner of his mouth and fished out a lighter from his jeans. "Shayna liked me." He eyed me with a half smile. "If you know what I mean." He held the lighter up to the edge of the cigarette. "But she never liked the idea of the recreation complex, Ace. And when things . . . hit the skids with her, she told Benny she didn't want him to do it."

I wasn't sure if I'd ever met another human being so annoying. He talked in circles, he called me Ace, he wore the most ridiculous toupee I'd ever seen, and he dressed like a goofy Elvis.

He lit the end of the cigarette and inhaled deeply. His cheeks bulged for a moment, and the color rose in his face. Then he spiraled into a coughing fit an asthmatic would've been appalled at.

The cigarette fell out of his mouth, and if I'd been inside the restaurant and heard him, I would've thought someone was attacking him, his hacking was so loud.

Fake hair and a fake smoker, too, apparently.

He got the coughing fit under control and smashed the cigarette under his boot.

"Are you telling me you had an affair with

Shayna?" I asked when it appeared he was no longer dying from smoke inhalation.

He grabbed his jacket from the hood of the wagon, extracted another cigarette from an interior pocket, and wisely stuck it behind his ear rather than lighting it. "I'm not telling you anything, Ace." The half smile appeared again as he slipped the jacket on. "But that girl was a tornado in the sack."

I wanted to believe he was lying. If you offered any woman the chance to sleep with this guy and, say, Bob the cat, I thought most would've taken their time making their decision before settling on Bob. What in the world could Shayna possibly have found attractive about him? For that matter, why would Benny have even been friends with the guy, much less handed over thirty thousand to him?

"So you in?" Odell Barnabas asked. "'Cause I'm really ready to get goin' on this baby, Ace. And you don't wanna miss the ride."

"Gonna have to think on it, Odell," I said, heading for my minivan. "Gonna have to think on it."

"Don't give it too much thought," Odell called after me. "Too much thinkin' will get you in trouble, Ace."

If that were true, Odell Barnabas would probably go his entire life without getting in trouble.

22

It was Carly's late day at school, when she stayed an extra hour and had lunch at Rettler-Mott. Julianne and I had made plans to have an early lunch. I thought it was a ploy to keep me out of trouble. If that was truly her intent, we should've had breakfast.

One of the reasons we've stayed in Rose Petal is its proximity to Dallas. A twenty-minute drive to the south and we're in the middle of a big city. Rose Petal had changed because of its location north of the city. When I was growing up, it felt like a small town. But as Dallas expanded, so did the suburbs and the amount of time people were willing to spend on the road commuting. As a result, Rose Petal was having an identity crisis. It was attempting to hang on to its small town feel while coming to the realization that small towns don't have populations that are growing by the day.

After Julianne graduated from A&M, she'd gone to UT for law school, something that many folks found sacrilege, myself included. You're an Aggie or you're a Longhorn. No one is an AgHorn. Nonetheless, she graduated from law school at UT and immediately went to work for a small firm in Dallas. The small firm had gone from small to medium to large in the decade she'd been there, and she'd been smart to stick around. At thirty-five, she was already a managing partner at Gaylin, Olson, and Armstrong.

Her office was over in the Park Cities, a stretch of real estate comprised of both Highland Park and University Park, near SMU. It was prime digs, the land of old Dallas wealth. As a kid, it seemed worlds away. It still felt odd that Julianne worked there every day.

I was stopped at a red light a block away from the office and I could see her out front, talking on her cell phone.

A decade and a half ago, during my first year at A&M, I'd seen her standing outside a bar, talking on a pay phone. Dark hair pulled back in a ponytail. Denim skirt and a long-sleeve blouse. Great eyes, even better legs.

I was with some buddies and waved them on into the bar ahead of me. Too tough to pick up girls when your friends were behind them, making obscene gestures.

She hung up the phone as I approached and looked me up and down, her expression telling me she wasn't terribly impressed.

I pointed up to the sign above the bar. "This a fun place?"

"If you like beer and being groped," she replied.

"I like beer, but I *love* being groped."

She didn't want to laugh, but she couldn't fight it off. She gave me the once-over again. "You're a football player, right? You look like one, all big and . . . dopey looking. Should I be swooning?"

"I am not a football player," I said, the words stinging even as they came out. "I am dopey looking, though. The swooning choice is all yours."

She smiled. Teeth that matched the eyes and legs. "I think you're lying. Besides, I know who you are."

That caught me by surprise. "I wouldn't lie about being dopey looking. And how do you know me?"

"You *couldn't* lie about being dopey looking. We went to high school together." She locked her eyes on me. "You are Deuce Winters, football star to the masses."

I bent down and rolled up the pant leg of my jeans, exposing the foot-long scar that ran diagonally across my right knee, and tried desperately to remember this girl. I was having a hard time believing I didn't remember her.

"Ouch," she said.

"Yeah. You really went to Rose Petal?"

She nodded and brushed the hair away from her face. "I was two years behind you."

That made some sense. In high school you paid attention to your peers, not the ones nipping at your heels. But girls were a different story. It didn't matter what year they were. It only mattered how hot they were, and this girl would've been hotter than hot as a toddler.

"You don't remember me, do you?" she asked, amused.

I thought about lying, trying to bluff my way through the conversation. But she seemed too sharp for any of my tricks.

"I don't," I said. "I can't believe it and I'm sorry."

I let the pant leg fall down and stood back up.

"Do you show your scar to everyone you meet?" she asked.

"Just the ones who accuse me of being dopey looking."

"Hardly an accusation when you copped to it."

I laughed. Loudly. She was knockout gorgeous and funny and a wiseass. A sucker combination. *How* had I missed this girl in Rose Petal?

"I take it you don't like this place," I said, nodding at the bar.

"Not particularly."

"Any place you do like?"

She thought for a moment; then her eyes lit up. "Dairy Queen."

"They don't serve beer at DQ."

"No. But they make those big peanut butter parfaits that have an alcoholic effect on me."

I nodded. "Okay. Would you like to go to Dairy Queen and have a peanut butter parfait? On me?"

She raise a pretty eyebrow. "There's usually no groping at Dairy Queen. Can you live with that?"

I pretended to think about it. "For one night, I guess I can."

She stuck out her hand. "I'm Julianne Willis."

I felt my jaw start to fall. "Willis? Tony Willis's little sister?"

"One and the same."

Tony was a year ahead of me in school, but we'd played football together since junior high. I vaguely remembered a little sister sitting on the sidelines. The last time I remembered seeing her, she was wearing glasses and had her nose in a book.

I really was a dope.

I shook her hand. Soft, warm, made my heart flutter. "Deuce."

"I already told you I knew that," she said, squeezing my hand. "It's a silly name, by the way."

"Not sillier than my real name," I said. "Eldrick. Like my dad. I was the second. Hence, the deuce."

"Clever."

"I can't believe I don't remember you," I said.

"Well, Deuce. Play your cards right and I might not hold it against you. And maybe there will be a little groping in your future."

We'd been together ever since. It was clichéd and silly and cutesy and lame. But Julianne was my best friend, and I thought of our first real meeting every time I saw her standing in the distance.

I pulled up to the curb, and she got in, still yammering on her phone.

"Yeah, yeah, yeah," she said, rolling her eyes. "I'm not impressed, John. We're planning on filing the motion, and I think you should plan on running for cover." She listened intently, a thin smile spreading across her face. "Let me know then." She shut the phone and dropped it in her purse and looked at me. "Hello."

"Hello. Having fun?"

"Always. I'm suckering that guy so badly, he's gonna wanna find a new job when I'm done with him," she said gleefully. "I am so good at this lawyering stuff."

I checked the mirror and pulled away from the curb. "I never had a doubt."

"So. What's up with you?"

"I'm taking you out tomorrow night," I said.

"Really?" she asked, surprised. "Where? And, more importantly, why?"

"How would you like to go to a witch hunt?"

She clicked her teeth together, then blew air quietly between them. "Before you tell me about the rest of our date, can I get some food in my stomach?"

"Your wish is my command."

"Right."

We found a table at a little BBQ joint a couple of blocks away, and she'd polished off half of her brisket sandwich before she could look me in the eye again. "So. This witch hunt. I'm assuming you're the witch?"

"I'm thinking I should wear a hat and bring a broom," I said, wiping sauce from my chin. "Really make a statement."

"I think you should stop trying to be funny and just tell me what's going on."

I told her about the meeting at school.

To my surprise, she didn't chastise me like she had the previous day for doing stupid things. She was actually more irritated than I was.

"Let me get this right," she said, picking up her sandwich, then dropping it back on the plate. "The WORMS think they can just remove you for no reason?"

"Well, they think they have a reason."

She made a face like I'd fed her a spoonful of dirt. "Please. Even if you were under investigation—and to this point, as far as we know, you are not—and even with the restraining order on file, none of that has anything to do with you providing snacks to a roomful of three-year-olds on occasion."

"I tried to tell them that."

Julianne bit into her sandwich like she was biting

off Sharon Ann's head. "They have so picked the wrong man to fight with."

I puffed out my chest, grateful for my wife's belief in me. "Well, thank you. I think so too. If they think they can just push me around . . ."

"Because they have no idea what they are going to have to deal with when I get in that room," she said, stabbing the air with her fork.

"You?" I asked. "When you get in that room?"

She nodded and stared at the fork, thoughtfully. "I just might make them cry. Every single one of them."

I finished off my own sandwich. "You don't think I can handle this myself?"

She threw her napkin on the table. "Of course I think you can handle this. But I think I might be able to help." She shook her head, narrowing her eyes. "These broads are gonna be so sorry they picked on my husband."

I wasn't entirely sure I was comfortable with her fighting my preschool battles. But after getting a load of the look in her eyes at that moment, I wasn't prepared to do anything but agree with my awesome, awesome wife.

23

I dropped Julianne back at her office and went back to pick Carly up at school. I didn't avoid the stares from Sharon Ann, Deborah, and the other WORMS, instead smiling happily at them. They immediately went into whispering mode, clearly unnerved by their inability to intimidate me. If that made them nervous, I almost felt sorry for them, knowing that Julianne was coming for them.

Almost.

Carly and I walked out of school, holding hands. I was carrying her backpack while she clutched onto the papers she was bringing home for the day. Nearly every afternoon she came home with a handful of construction paper, drawings, and announcements, representing all the work she did in class that day. She rarely gave them up before she reached the car, as if carrying them showed everyone that she had, indeed, completed one more day of school and no one was taking that away from her.

She jumped into the backseat and shoved the

stack of papers in my face. "These are for you, Daddy."

I buckled her into her seat. "Thank you sooo much."

"You're welcome."

I scanned the papers as I walked around to the driver's side. A drawing of a person that was all head with a microscopic body. Next month's calendar. And a flyer for swimming lessons.

At Tough Tykes.

Julianne and I had discussed that it was probably time to get her into swimming. Carly loved the water, and we spent nearly every day during the summer at one of the couple of community pools in our neighborhood. I had been able to teach her a little, and she could doggy-paddle her way to safety if she absolutely had to. But it was time for her to learn how to do it correctly.

I climbed into the van, stuck the key in the ignition, and weighed my options. We hadn't really discussed where she was going to take lessons, and I had yet to do any investigating. Going to Tough Tykes would most likely draw my wife's ire, given the warning she'd already given me about steering clear of anything Benny related. But it wasn't like I was going there for any other reason than to just check out the possibility of swimming lessons for our daughter, right?

As I pointed the van in the direction of Tough Tykes, I knew I'd have to come up with something better than that before Julianne got home.

Like not even telling her we went there. That would probably have been the smart thing to do.

24

Tough Tykes was in a newer area of Rose Petal. High-end shops were being built by the half dozen, and expansive homes were going up to make sure the shops had people shopping in them. The denizens of Rose Petal were divided on how they felt about this. Half wanted the town to remain a town, the small outpost of Dallas where everyone knew each other's name. But the other half, those that weren't Texas natives and had moved to the area for jobs in Dallas, was all for it. Rose Petal was the perfect bedroom community, and they saw no reason why they should have to leave the town to shop at Target, Wal-Mart, or Home Depot. Good schools, relatively safe—my minivan excepted—and less than half an hour to the big city.

I was somewhere in the middle. I did like the small-town aspect of Rose Petal growing up. But I also knew that all those new homes, and businesses were good for the town, wouldn't let it die off like some of those other Texas hideaways out to the west.

We had in fact bought one of those new homes and I knew some folks felt like we'd gone over to the dark side. It didn't bother me that much.

Plus, I liked shopping at Target.

But Tough Tykes was out in a field of new development, with signs promising more restaurants and shops to come. Tough Tykes itself looked more like an airplane hangar with giant windows than anything else. It was a long, rectangular building with its name emblazoned on all four sides in brilliant red and black letters. An American flag, a Texas flag, and a Tough Tykes flag waved in the wind atop the structure. A massive parking lot fronted the building, usually filled with SUVs and other modes of toting kids around town. There was actually a rack at the front of the building where you could lock up your baby jogger.

So smart.

"What is this, Daddy?" Carly asked as we turned in.

"Remember how I told you about taking swimming lessons?"

There was a pause, indicating she clearly didn't remember. "Yes."

"Well, they teach swimming here, and I wanna go find out about classes."

"For me?"

"Yep."

"Do you know how to swim, Daddy?"

"Yep."

"Good. 'Cause I wanna take lessons all by myself."

Wow. Only like fifteen more years of hearing things like that. Awesome.

We parked the van, got out, and Carly was already jittery with excitement, pulling on my hand as we crossed the lot.

The lobby itself was a showcase for the whole facility. It was designed to feel like you were entering a stadium or sports arena—turnstiles, pictures of smiling, active kids, a massive counter staffed with numerous fresh-faced-looking college-aged kids in red and black golf shirts, music blaring, and a thirty-foot-high ceiling that made the entire area feel twice as large as it actually was.

We made our way over to the counter, where a young girl with long blond hair greeted us as if she'd been waiting her whole life for us to arrive.

"Hello!" she said, looking first at me, then Carly. "Welcome to Tough Tykes. I'm Mandy. How can I help you?"

Carly put her chin up on the counter. "I wanna swim."

Mandy smiled at her, a laser beam of enthusiasm emanating from her expression. "I'll bet you're a good swimmer."

"We'd actually like to get some information on swimming lessons," I said.

"Have you visited Tough Tykes before?"

"We have not."

She gathered up several pieces of paper, came around the desk, and held her hand out to Carly. "Well, let's go take a look around, shall we?"

Carly beamed and grabbed her hand.

Mandy was smooth. She had already ingratiated herself with Carly before I could say we had somewhere else to be or gently deflect her sales pitch and quickly get the information I wanted. Carly might have liked her, but I was wary.

As Mandy led us around, I had to admit that the facility was quite impressive. There were two full-length gymnasiums dedicated solely to basketball. Boys and girls filled them both, running drills. Staffers about Mandy's age put them through their paces. There were two massive multipurpose gymnasiums that were mainly used for gymnastics but could also host birthday parties. A large dojo housed martial arts classes. There was a strength training area, an indoor batting cage, and another room dedicated to cheerleading and dance. Mandy showed us the locker-room area before bringing us to the indoor pool.

"And this is where Miss Carly will take her lessons," Mandy said, still clutching Carly's hand and smiling in my direction.

She might have been young, but someone had schooled her well in sales techniques. Make friends with the kid, smile at the dad, and act as if we're already signed up. Smooth.

The pool was junior Olympic in length, with cutouts every few feet along the sides, where the classes could sit on steps. Four kids max to a class, and if all went well, they could hit the giant dinosaur slides at the far end before class was over. A small viewing area ran behind a wall of glass at the far end, so the kids could see Mom or Dad but couldn't jump out of the pool and cling to them.

The pool, like everything else, was impressive.

"Daddy, I wanna swim! I wanna swim!" Carly clamored, jumping up and down, pulling on Mandy's arm.

Mandy handed me the paperwork. "All of the class information is listed, along with the prices. You'll be looking at the Little Mermaid classes for Carly."

"I wanna be a mermaid!" Carly yelled.

"And let me take you back up front," Mandy said, squeezing Carly's hand. "I've got a little surprise for you."

Carly nearly burst, she was so excited.

Back at the desk, Mandy found a tiny toy mermaid and handed it to Carly like it was the lost Ark. "You take very special care of this mermaid, and you remember to bring her back with you when you come for your first lesson."

Carly nodded, holding the mermaid as if she'd just been presented with a diamond. Made of cotton candy.

Smooth, that Mandy.

Mandy smiled at me. "Any questions that I can answer?"

I tried hard to think of something she didn't cover on our tour, but failed. Mandy was good at her job.

"I think you hit it all," I said. "Thank you."

A good-looking guy materialized next to Mandy behind the counter. About six feet tall, athletic build, tan skin. Probably in his fifties, but had that "I'm totally in shape so I seem younger" look. Close-cropped dark hair. Crisp red and black golf shirt.

If possible, Mandy seemed to brighten even more.

"Howdy, folks," he said. "Mandy tell you everything you need to know?" He smiled down at Carly. "You have a good time, sweetheart?"

Carly nodded enthusiastically, still clutching the mermaid.

He nodded, happy to see her response, then moved his eyes back to me. “And you, Mr. Winters? You like what you see?”

He knew my name and that surprised me. “I’m sorry. Have we met?”

“No, sir, we haven’t, but I’d be a fool not knowing Deuce Winters if he walked into my place.” He held out his hand. “I’m Jimmy Landry.”

25

"My brother was a coach over at Bartonville your junior and senior years," Jimmy Landry said. "Defensive coordinator. You made his life miserable."

We were sitting in his office, back behind the main desk area. Carly was sitting in my lap, playing with her new mermaid.

"Sorry about that," I said.

He waved his hand in the air. "Please. You were a heckuva player."

"Did you coach?"

"Nah, just a fan, like everyone else." He grinned. "Too busy making plans for things like this place."

I nodded and took a quick look around the office. It was square and medium-sized, nothing terribly distinguished about it. There was nothing that said it was the owner's office, other than the several plaques with Landry's name on the walls, touting his community service. It was a room to work in, not a room to show off his ego.

"So what'd you think of the place?" he asked, leaning back in his chair.

"Pretty amazing," I said truthfully. "You've got just about everything a kid could want under one roof."

"We're trying," he said. "I'm always looking for things to add, things that people want for their kids."

"Seems like you're pretty much the main game in Rose Petal," I said.

"So far," he said, then shrugged. "Somebody'll come along soon enough and try to copy us. Lot of families in this area. Competition's good. Keeps us on our toes. Hopefully, though, we've got some loyalty with the folks who are using us now."

"I heard someone was already planning to do something similar."

He stared at me, his expression blank for a moment; then amused recognition washed over his face. "You mean that crazy Barnabas fella?"

I nodded.

Landry laughed. "Well, I guess. But I have to tell you, at the risk of sounding pretty pompous, I did not take that guy too seriously."

"Why not?"

"Have you seen him?"

I laughed. "Point taken."

Landry laughed, too. "Okay, maybe that's a little unfair. I don't know him, so I shouldn't be calling him crazy. But he had no clue what he was talking about, and it was just impossible to think of him as competition."

"So he did come talk to you?"

"He did," Landry said, nodding. "Couple of months ago. Wanted to know if we bought the building and had it brought here from somewhere else or if we built it." He chuckled at the memory. "Like I said, hard to take him seriously."

"You ever meet his partners?" I asked.

"Didn't know he had any. But for my sake, I hope Barnabas is the brains of the operation."

"Gotcha." I looked at Carly. She was getting antsy in my lap, fidgeting. I shifted her into my left arm and stood. "We've gotta head out."

Landry stood and put his hands on his hips. "What do you do for a living, Deuce?"

"I stay at home," I said, nodding at Carly. "Take care of her."

"That's great," he said, seeming to genuinely mean it. "Let me ask you this, then. Would you have any interest in doing a little coaching?"

That took me by surprise. "Here?"

He nodded. "Yeah. We're going to run some sports camps this summer. One- and two-week deals. I'd love to have somebody like you working the football camps. I was going to call you and introduce myself and invite you in, so when I saw you and your daughter up front there, I just figured I'd go ahead and extend the offer now."

He didn't know it, but he was pushing the right button. Since I'd left the high school, I hadn't really missed the teaching or the administrative tasks that came along with the classroom. But I missed being out on the field with the kids.

"Don't say no today," he said, holding up a hand. "Think it over. We could work around your schedule, and you could set it up any way you want. But I'd love to have you if you have any interest."

I offered my hand. "Thanks, Jimmy. I'll definitely think about it."

He shook my hand and walked us back out front. Mandy waved good-bye to Carly, who waved back like Mandy was her best friend ever.

"Hope we see you again, Deuce," Jimmy Landry said.

Based on Carly's impression of Tough Tykes, I was pretty sure he could count on that.

26

We stopped at the park on the way home, and I let Carly play for a while. Running around did her good and left her less wound up for the rest of the day. Sitting in the sun and watching her did the same for me. Watching her sprint from slide to swing to tunnel, wide-eyed and sweaty, convinced me that the American working public would be better served if one of those monstrous play apparatuses was installed in every business park in the country. It would serve everyone well for grown men and women to spend a few minutes running around in dress clothes in the middle of their workday and coming down the giant twisty slide. There was no equal as a stress buster, and the exercise would be an added benefit.

If I could find a company that did that, I just might consider going back to work when Carly was in school full-time.

When she was sufficiently worn out, we headed home, and after the tiniest bit of resistance, she went down for a nap.

As I came downstairs from her room, I saw a car

parked across the street through our front window. A green Chevy Impala. I didn't recognize it, yet it rang a bell somewhere in my head. I went to the window and stared at it for a moment. I didn't see a driver, and it didn't look new, as if one of our neighbors had just purchased it. I assumed it was just someone visiting one of our neighbors in the cul-de-sac, but there was just something about it that nagged at me.

I went to the kitchen, thinking I was just being paranoid.

I took several pieces of chicken out of the freezer to barbecue for dinner, did the morning dishes, and emptied the dishwasher from the night before. I pulled the laundry from the dryer, folded it and put it away, and started another load that had somehow materialized overnight. If there was anything that was a true surprise about staying home, it was the way dirty clothes appeared in the clothes basket at an exponential rate. As if people lived in the walls, tried on all our clothes while we were out, and then dumped them in the basket, just to mess with us.

When you stay home, you have time to think about things like this.

I grabbed a wire brush that I used to clean the grill and went to open the back screen door. It stuck, and I shoved it hard to get it to swing open.

And I heard someone grunt.

The guy was on his back, holding his nose. And I'm not sure what the most appropriate term for him was.

Midget? Dwarf?

He was about three feet tall, wearing jeans and a plaid button-down shirt that would've fit Carly. A gray fedora was askew on his small, fat head.

"What the hell are you doing?" I asked, because "What the hell are you?" would've been totally inappropriate.

He scrambled to his feet and tried to take off. I grabbed him by the back of his shirt collar. He swung his hand around, slapping at mine.

"Let go!" he said, his voice much deeper than I expected. "Let go of my shirt."

I swung him around so I was between him and his escape route and let go. He stumbled against the back of the house, then turned around.

His long, pointed nose was red from where I'd hit him with the door. His features were all too big for his face, and his ears stuck out like wings. He brushed himself off with his tiny hands and stubby fingers.

"What the hell are you doing in my backyard?" I asked.

"You're Deuce Winters, correct?" he asked, again in that voice that was more Barry White than Munchkin.

"You've got ten seconds to tell me who you are," I said, ignoring his question. "Or I'm calling the cops."

He held out his hands, encouraging me to slow down. "Easy, dude. We're cool."

There was nothing cool about finding a midget or a dwarf or a strange guy in my backyard.

He reached into his back pocket and produced a wallet. I was surprised that it was the same size as mine. He extracted a business card and held it out to me.

The bold, embossed lettering read VICTOR ANTHONY DOOLITTLE. PRIVATE INVESTIGATOR. NO INVESTIGATION IS TOO SMALL.

I held back on the urge to ask him how he came up with that slogan. "You're an investigator?"

"I am," he said, nodding and adjusting the fedora. "And you are Deuce Winters, correct?"

"Yeah."

He laughed. "Good. Hate to think I've been following the wrong guy all day."

"You've been following me?"

"Yeah. You really need to pay attention to the world around you."

I knew I would've remembered him if I'd seen him. "That's your car out front?"

"So you were paying attention a little."

"Why are you following me?"

"I can't reveal that, sir," he said, shaking his head sadly. "My employer would not appreciate that."

"How would your employer like it if I put you on my BBQ and grilled you?"

His eyes flashed with anger. "Look, pal, I understand you're angry at finding me back here. But if you wanna joke about my size, I'll kick your ass."

I'm six-four. He was three-six, maybe. I doubted that he could lay his hand on my butt, much less his foot, without thc aid of a step stool.

"You're on my property, and now you're threatening me," I said, trying not to take the low road. So to speak. "I'm calling the cops."

He jumped into a karate stance, his small hands slicing through the air. "Good luck getting through me to your phone. It'll never happen." He chopped the air some more and curled his lips into a snarl.

I lifted my leg, put my foot in his belly, and pushed. He slammed back into the house and fell to the deck.

"Wow," I said. "Thanks for not chopping my leg off."

I reached for the door, but he grabbed for my leg, tugging with all the strength of a large cat. I shot my leg out, and he tumbled off the deck onto my lawn.

On one hand, I felt bad. He was small and I was not. I had never been a bully and had no interest in being one. Yet if he were adult size, our confrontation could've been a lot uglier. You didn't just walk into someone's backyard without permission.

But now he was lying in the grass on his back, and I felt like I'd just taken his lunch money.

I stepped off the deck and leaned over him. "Are you all right?"

He reached up suddenly, grabbed my shirt and, with strength that surprised me this time, yanked me down. I lost my balance and fell forward, somersaulting over him.

He was on my back immediately, his stubby arms wrapped around my neck, pulling back on me like I was a horse and he was a jockey.

"What do you think now, tough guy?" he asked, wheezing. "Wanna put me on the barbecue now?"

I got to my hands and knees and rolled over, pinning him beneath me. His hands relaxed around my neck, and he started kicking and yelling.

"Get off! Get off!" he screamed into my back. "I can't breathe."

I leaned back a little harder, smashing him into the grass. No more Mr. Nice Dad.

"You want me off, start talking," I said, laying my arms out flat to keep myself leveraged. "Or I'll turn you into an ugly little pancake."

His hands were now in the small of my back, pushing. He might as well have been trying to shove a refrigerator off his body. I was going nowhere.

"All right, all right," he groaned. "Just get off me so I can breathe."

I pressed down hard one more time, heard him grunt; then I rolled off.

He sighed and took a couple of big breaths, glancing at me. "You coulda killed me."

"Keep that in mind."

His fedora had fallen off in the scrum, exposing a bald pate. He rubbed a hand over his skull, now staring up at the sky. "I'm just doing a routine background check on you," he explained, shrugging his little shoulders. "Nothing personal."

"Background check? For what? For who?"

He cleared his throat and attempted to compose himself. "It's a routine procedure. It's a background check, sir."

"I know what a background check is. Why are you doing one on me?"

"I can't divulge any more, sir," Victor Doolittle said. "Client-investigator privilege."

"There's no such thing."

He sat up. "Whatever. I'm not telling you who my client is."

I pushed myself to my knees. I couldn't decide if I was angry, amused, or had mistakenly ingested some sort of hallucinogenic.

"So if you're gonna call the fuzz, do it," he said. "I got places to be."

The fuzz? Seriously?

Calling the police was about the last thing I wanted to do. With my luck, Willie Bell would show up and turn the whole thing into my fault. I'd had enough of him and law enforcement in the previous couple of days.

"Here's the deal," I finally said. "You tell me who hired you and I let you go. You don't wanna tell me, I will pick you up, put you in my trunk, and drive you straight to the cops."

The anger flared again in his eyes. "Hey, dude, I already told you . . ."

"Save it," I said, holding out a hand. "Or I'll steamroll you again. You make the call."

His mouth puckered and he glared at me. Then his eyes shifted past me, and he raised an eyebrow. "What the hell is that?"

I turned to look.

And got sucker punched in the last place a male of any age wants to be sucker punched.

The air whooshed out of me, and I felt stomach cramps forming in my gut as my hands cupped over my area that shall not be named.

Victor Anthony Doolittle was on his feet, his tiny legs flailing in every direction as he sprinted out of my yard, his small middle finger high in the air.

27

"When you say 'dwarf,' you just mean 'really small guy,' right?" Julianne asked.

"No. I mean like Happy, Dopey, and Jerky."

"Jerky wasn't one of the Seven Dwarfs."

"He should've been."

We were upstairs getting ready for bed. Julianne had gotten home late from work, and Carly and I were finishing our dinner when she'd arrived. The rest of the night had been disjointed: as I got Carly ready for her bath and bed, Julianne sat at the dinner table, eating her chicken and finishing up some paperwork.

We had a lot of nights like that. Julianne did her best to get home at a reasonable hour in order to spend some time with Carly in the evenings, but sometimes it just didn't work out. Julianne didn't work a nine-to-five job, and sometimes her schedule didn't lend itself to normal family time in the evenings. So sometimes we spent the whole night playing catch-up.

Julianne had gotten Carly into bed and had read

her her story, and I was just now getting around to telling her about Victor Anthony Doolittle.

"And he wore a hat?"

"Probably to make himself look taller."

She finished her flossing and picked up the electric toothbrush. "I think they prefer to be called little people. You should've called the police."

I scrubbed a washcloth over my face. "And said what? 'Help. There's a small man in my backyard'?"

"He was technically trespassing." She pushed the button on the toothbrush and it vibrated to life.

She was right. My not calling the cops probably had more to do with ego than any other reason I was going to toss out there. And besides being in my backyard, he hadn't really done anything wrong. I didn't like that he was following me or doing his supposed background check, but those things weren't necessarily against the law.

Jules finished with the electric toothbrush, plucked the head off, and handed the base to me. I stuck the head that was mine on and blasted my teeth with waves of vibration, still pissed off that I had fallen for the old "Hey! Look over there!" trick.

And then I started laughing.

"What?" Julianne asked, watching me in the mirror.

I started laughing harder, toothpaste leaking out of my mouth.

"What?" Julianne asked again, laughing only because I was laughing.

I shut off the toothbrush and spit into the sink, still laughing. "His legs. They were like small pinwheels when he ran off."

We stood there for a few moments, laughing like fools.

When we'd finally let the giggle fit pass, we crawled into bed.

"Why would someone be doing a background check on me?" I asked.

She turned off the light and slid across the bed next to me, wrapping me up in her arms. "I have no idea. That part is odd."

"That part."

"Okay. The private eye midget is odd, too."

"I'd say."

She snuggled in tighter against my chest. "But I don't know about the background check. I can't think of anything that we know of that would require it."

More than anything, that was what had been bugging me the most. We weren't applying for a loan, refinancing the house, or anything else I could think of that would cause anyone to be checking me out. I couldn't decide if he'd been telling the truth or just trying to bluff me. Was he there for another reason? The whole fifteen-minute confrontation had been the strangest of my life.

Julianne started shaking against my chest, and I could tell she was giggling.

"What?" I asked.

Her giggle turned into a full-blown, body-rattling laugh. She somehow got the word "pinwheel" out of her mouth, and then I started laughing.

We lay there in the dark, laughing, for quite some time.

28

I woke the next morning in a surprisingly good mood, given my confrontation with the midget PI and my impending engagement with the WORMS.

One of the things that I missed about coaching was the thing that I missed most when my days as a football player ended. I loved the thrill of competition as a player, and though I had doubted that it would be the same as a coach, I found it to be greater. Having to stand on the sidelines, exhorting my players to do what we were asking them to do, proved much more exciting than I'd ever imagined. And when they did execute and I could see them putting to use what I'd taught them, that turned out to be a much bigger adrenaline rush than anything I'd ever experienced as a player.

So while I was angry at the reason for the showdown, a small spark of excitement over the emergency meeting was percolating in my gut.

Carly's and my first stop for the day was her ballet and tap class. It was held in a small studio in the middle of town, and she'd been attending for about six months, and much to my chagrin, she loved it. Julianne could complain all she wanted about how I dressed her, but Carly was showing plenty of signs that she was all girly girl.

I dropped her at the hour-long class and took the opportunity to walk a block up to the Rose Petal police station, which was nothing more than a small office at the end of the strip mall that housed the dance studio, a sandwich shop, and the station.

Cedric was sitting out front in an aluminum beach chair.

"Keeping the town safe?" I asked.

"As long as I know where you are, seems most folks will think we're all safe," he retorted, adjusting his sheriff's hat to block the sun.

"You wanna cuff me? In case I try anything?"

"Naw. Don't feel like getting up."

Since he'd been forced into his mostly ceremonial position, Cedric spent most days in the beach chair, drinking his coffee and waiting for something to happen. Usually he didn't have to move much from the chair, other than to hit the bathroom and find some lunch. He tried to act like it didn't bother him, but those of us that knew him well understood it irritated him greatly and it sucked to see him relegated to watching traffic from the beach chair.

"You know a guy named Victor Doolittle?" I asked, falling into the chair next to him.

"The midget? Sure, I know Victor."

"He's really an investigator?"

"And a royal pain in the butt," Cedric said, shaking his head. "Annoying, abrasive, and a justified little man's complex, which I suppose you'd expect. Lives down in Dallas but tends to hang out here, because he thinks people got more money up here. Which they do."

"He's legit, though? As an investigator?"

He raised the silver coffee thermos to his mouth for a moment, then nodded. "He's legit. And, to be fair, from what I've been told, he's actually decent at what he does." He cocked an eye at me. "Why? You lookin' to hire that penguin for something?"

"No. He came to see me. Says he's doing some sort of background check on me but wouldn't tell me for who."

"Probably those ladies at Carly's school," he said, a sly smile forming on his face.

That had definitely crossed my mind. But the time frame didn't make sense. If the guy was doing a true background check, it would take more than a day or two. The emergency meeting was tonight. He wouldn't have had the time to get them whatever he was looking for.

"Doing a background check isn't illegal, Deuce," Cedric said, circling the thermos with both hands. "They happen all the time."

"I know. It just seemed weird, with everything going on."

"You think it's related to Benny?"

"Timing of it seems pretty coincidental."

He thought about that for a moment, then frowned like he thought I was wrong. "The timing is coincidental. But from a law enforcement standpoint, the only person who'd be looking into your background regarding Benny would be Willie Bell." He processed his own words, then shook his head firmly. "And he wouldn't hire that out. There's no reason. He can do it himself, and he can do it faster."

That made sense. And Bell seemed like the kind of guy who would enjoy doing that stuff all by himself.

"If you're looking for something to tie it to," Cedric offered, "I think you'd be better off thinking about your restraining order."

"How's that?"

He sipped from the coffee. "If somebody is looking to give a restraining order some teeth, they have to go looking for the teeth."

"I'm not following, Cedric."

He peered over the thermos at me. "The restraining order is only temporary. It will expire. If Shayna wants it to stick against you, she's gonna need to show cause."

I shifted in the uncomfortable chair and watched a few cars drive past us. I still didn't understand the restraining order, yet I couldn't get close enough to Shayna to ask her about it. If Cedric was right and she had hired an investigator to cement her claim, then she was serious, which, until that moment, I didn't think she was. I had played my visit to her house over in my head a dozen times and kept coming to the same conclusion.

I didn't do anything wrong.

"I'm not saying that's a sure thing," Cedric said. "But if you're looking for a reason as to why that little munchkin might be digging in your garden, that might fit." He shrugged his shoulders. "I'll keep an ear open on it."

"Thanks," I said. "Got another question for you."

"Good Lord, Deuce. This what stay-at-home dads get to do all day? Go around asking questions?"

I laughed. "No. You know the guy that runs Tough Tykes? Jimmy Landry?"

"Little bit. Why?"

"I don't know. Not what I was expecting. Met him yesterday. Seemed like a good guy."

"What were you expecting?"

"Not sure. Just not what he was. He offered me a job."

Cedric pushed the brim of the hat up a little higher. "Doesn't he know how busy *this* job keeps you? Who would I chat with if you took another job?"

"Coaching," I said, ignoring the jab. "He's running some summer football camps, and he asked if I'd be interested in helping out."

"Well, that guy's pretty smart, then."

"Why's that?"

"If he can put your name on his flyers in this town, that oughta sell out his camps in about three seconds."

"I doubt that."

Cedric frowned. "Son, I have always appreciated your modesty. Your parents did right by you. But if you think the words *Deuce Winters* and *football* don't still get people fired up around here, you are sadly mistaken."

On cue, my knee throbbed and I rubbed it, like I wanted to rub away the memories, too.

"People will go nut crazy to get their kids on a field with you," Cedric said. "And don't take me the wrong way. I think that's a good thing. Kids would be lucky to have you screaming and yelling at them."

It was a nice thing for him to say.

"Of course, maybe them ladies at the school might try to have you removed from there, too."

That, however, wasn't so nice.

29

Carly and I dropped off some clothes at the cleaners, stopped at the bank to deposit a check, and then headed home.

Billy Caldwell was waiting in our driveway.

We really needed to look into moving to a gated community. Dwarves yesterday, jerks today.

Carly immediately recognized him from when he was in our living room several days prior. “That’s that man with the boots.”

“Yes, it is,” I said, unbuckling her seat belt.

Her little brows furrowed together. “I don’t like him.”

“Me either.”

She jumped out of the car and grabbed my hand. “Let’s go inside, Daddy.” She led me around the van.

Billy greeted us with a half wave. “Hello, Deuce.”

“Stay right there,” I said to him as Carly led me in a wide circle around him and up the steps to our front porch. I opened the front door and wriggled my hand free from hers. “I have to go talk to him. I’ll be in in a minute, okay?”

"I'll watch from in here," she said.

"That's fine. It'll just take a minute."

"Watch out for his boots, Daddy."

I left her behind the screen door, standing there with a serious look on her face, as if she might charge out and bite Billy in the shin if he tried anything shifty.

I hopped down the stairs and met Billy in the driveway. "What do you want?"

He looked past me, up at the house. "I was gonna apologize to your little girl, Deuce. For the other night."

"She doesn't like you, Billy," I said. "She's a smart kid. She doesn't need you apologizing to her."

His cheeks reddened, and he fiddled with the bright green tie knotted at his neck. The suit today was light gray with pinstripes; the shirt was a light green. The boots were still ugly.

"You don't need to be like that, Deuce," he said.

"I know I don't, but you just bring it out in me. What do you want, Billy?"

He reached into his jacket pocket and extracted a folded-up group of papers. He held them out to me. "Shayna's decided to go ahead with the lawsuit."

I took the papers but didn't look at them. "Julianne will get a kick out of these. I think she'll be happy, because it might be a chance for her to kick your ass in court."

He fiddled with the tie again. "Julianne doesn't handle civil suits like this."

"But you're special, Billy. She might just do it so she can embarrass you. Would give her a thrill, you know?"

He stuck his hands in his pockets and shuffled

the boots against the driveway. "I'm just here as a courtesy, Deuce. That's all."

"Was the restraining order a courtesy as well?"

He pursed his lips and rocked on his heels, a tiny spark in his dark eyes. "Shouldna gone botherin' her, Deuce."

"Bull," I said. "Shayna called me and asked me to come over. It was stupid of me to go over, but she asked. She knows it, I know it, and I'll bet everything I have that you know it."

He continued to rock, giving a tiny shrug, an ambivalent expression on his face.

"Why'd she file it, Billy? I didn't do anything, and you both know it. Whatever's going on here, it isn't gonna fly. If you think I'm gonna sit around and just take this garbage, you're wrong."

A slow smile spread across his face. "Same old Deuce. Arrogant and determined to right the wrongs of the world."

"Same old Billy," I said. "Jealous and weak."

The smile slithered off his face. It had been like that between us for almost two decades. He'd been the quarterback of our team in high school, a position that should've been the movie star role in our town. Billy Caldwell should've been the biggest man in town for his three years on the varsity and should've been able to run for mayor when he was done.

Only Billy handled it exactly the worst way you'd want to handle a situation like that. He got arrogant. Didn't realize that the key to getting the accolades was acting like you didn't deserve them. He thought he deserved them and told everyone just that. And it was a problem for him because he couldn't back it up. He was an average football player at best, lazy in his work habits and big in the mouth. It was a combination that didn't make him popular in Rose Petal and didn't make him popular in our locker room.

And when some of us started fielding offers from colleges to go play after high school, it stuck in his gut that those schools weren't looking at him. Burned a straight line right through him, and he blamed everyone but himself for it. We were stealing his thunder, we weren't helping his cause, and we were just lucky.

Twenty years later I could see it in his face. He hated that I had Julianne and Carly and my life. It bothered him. He was a low-rent ambulance chaser, and I wasn't. It all showed right there on his face in my driveway.

He pulled his hands out of his pockets and held them in front of himself, palms up. "Say what you want. But I think we can both agree I've got the upper hand at the moment."

"There is no upper hand, Billy," I said. "I didn't kill Benny, and I didn't do anything to Shayna. And if you think some lawsuit based on something that happened twenty years ago is gonna keep me awake at night, you are very, very wrong. But you keep pushing me and I'm gonna push back. Hard."

"Wish I had that on tape," he said. "Some folks might see that as a threat."

"Screw you."

"We can settle it all. Right here and now."

I laughed, thinking he wanted to fight. "An ass kicking in your thirties isn't gonna be any different than it was when we were kids."

His expression wavered a bit, but it didn't completely fold. "Not what I was talking about."

I didn't say anything.

"Shayna would be open to a settlement," he said.

"I'll bet she would be."

"Don't discount it, Deuce," Billy said. "You can make all this go away. You give me a number and we'll work from it."

"Two," I said.

His features scrunched together. "Two? Hundred? Thousand? Two what?"

"Two seconds to get the hell out of my driveway."

He started backing down the driveway.

"And if you wear those boots over here again, I'm calling animal control."

His mouth twitched in anger; he turned on those boots and got in his car.

A settlement? Did I look that stupid? There was zero doubt in my mind that he and Shayna had something going on and somehow I'd landed in the middle of it.

As I walked back up to the house and waved at Carly in the window, I was determined to find out what exactly I was in the middle of.

30

If I was going down, I was going to go down looking good.

Staying home with Carly did not call for many occasions to dress myself up. My work attire consisted mostly of shorts, T-shirts, and sandals. I shaved about every third day. The occasional A&M hat on my head. I would've looked silly wearing a three-piece suit to the park.

But I figured I better look like I was taking this whole thing seriously at Rettler-Mott, so I showered, shaved, and busted out the good stuff. The only suit I owned (navy and tailored), a Brooks Brothers pinpoint oxford (a gift from Julianne), a red and blue striped tie (stolen from my dad when I needed one for a dinner at Julianne's firm about a year prior, and never returned), and shiny black wing tips (knock-offs, not name brands, because dress shoes are stupidly expensive, and if I'm spending money on shoes, it's going to be on cool-looking running shoes.)

Dressed to impress.

I dropped Carly at my parents' house.

My father looked me up and down as she skittered past him into the house. "You look ready."

"I am," I said, standing tall.

"I meant you look ready to walk right into the coffin before they bury you. Stay nimble on your feet in case they try to shove you in."

Families are so awesome.

The first thing I noticed about the parking lot at Rettler-Mott was how crowded it was. I didn't like that. I expected there to be a few folks, but I wasn't looking to argue this out in front of a huge audience. I imagined most of the folks were simply there to be entertained.

The second thing I noticed was that Julianne had not yet arrived.

And the third thing I noticed, unfortunately, was Darlene Andrews.

She sashayed across the lot in my direction, her hair blotting out the moon and the stars. The only thing I saw in the sky was the giant white ribbon lifting her locks to new, superior heights.

"Is Julianne coming?" she asked, scanning the parking lot, then lasering her eyes back to me.

"She'll be here."

"Too bad," she mumbled.

"What?"

"Nothing." She linked her arm inside mine. "Are you nervous?"

I thought about uncoiling my arm from hers, knocking her to the ground, and making a run for it. But I was already in enough trouble. "I'm fine, Darlene."

"It's like a snake pit in there," she said, pushing

in closer to me than was necessary. "You remember that scene in *Raiders of the Lost Ark?* Where Indiana Jones has to go into that hole full of snakes?" She squeezed my arm. "They're like the snakes. And you are just like Indy."

Fantastic.

We reached the steps that descended down into the school, and I stopped. "I'm going to wait out here for Julianne."

The enthusiasm sagged out of her body. Not that anything ever really sagged on Darlene. "Oh. Would you like me to wait with you?" She squeezed my arm again. "For company. Or anything else."

"I'll be all right, Darlene," I said, disentangling our arms. "Go on in and get a good seat. I'll see you inside in a few minutes."

"Okay," she said, then pointed a hot pink fingernail at me. "Remember. You're Indiana!"

She went down the stairs and disappeared inside.

I lied to Darlene. I was nervous.

I paced back and forth to burn off some of that anxiety, waiting for Julianne.

A few people passed by on their way in, nodding or waving hello. I wondered whose side they were on. Indy's or the snakes'?

My cell phone buzzed in my pocket and I answered.

"I'm late," Julianne said. "I'm sorry."

"It's okay."

"I should be there in about five minutes. Is it crowded?"

I glanced at the full parking lot. "No. Just the entire town."

"You sound nervous."

"Well, Darlene just tried to push me down in the bushes and take advantage of me, so that may be it. She's pretty strong."

"So's her hair," Julianne said. "Damm red lights. Just relax. It's going to be fine. I did some reading today."

"Reading?"

"Of the school's bylaws. They're going to end up kissing my incredible ass by the time I'm done with them."

I had done no looking at the school's bylaws. I, in fact, didn't even know what bylaws were. It had never occurred to me to do anything like that, and now my anxiety level was hitting DEFCON 1. I was angry over being called out by the WORMS, but maybe I wasn't taking this seriously enough.

I strolled over near a bank of hedges that ran along the edge of the amphitheater. "Jules, I don't want you handling this for me."

"I know that," she said. "And you take your shot. I'll only get in the way if I need to." She paused. "I'm about thirty seconds away."

I didn't want her handling the whole thing. This was my fight and I wanted to defend myself, no matter how ridiculous the fight was. But it was good to know I had the best backup in the business if I needed her.

"I'm turning in right now," she said. "Where are you?"

I turned to the parking lot, my back to the hedge. I saw her Lexus coming in at the far end of the lot. "I'm here, in front of you on your left."

Her headlights flashed across the lot and hit

me in the eyes. I brought a hand across the top of my eyes.

"Deuce," she said. "Who is that behind you?"

"Nobody. It's the hedge."

"No. There's a person behind the hedge. Who is that?"

As I started to turn around, something hard and heavy thumped the back of my head. The phone fell out of my hand, and I dropped to my knees, stars dancing in my eyes.

One more shot to the back of the head and the stars dropped out of my eyes as the pavement came rushing at me before all the light disappeared.

31

My eyes opened, and I was looking up at Julianne, Darlene, and Sharon Ann.

Like Cinderella and her two wicked stepsisters.

"Don't move," Julianne said.

I pushed myself up to a sitting position.

"What happened?" Darlene asked, clutching my hand.

I reached around behind my head. A lump the size of an egg protruded from my skull. A dull throbbing was working its way from the inside of my head.

"Will you be okay for the emergency meeting?" Sharon Ann asked.

"Shut up, Sharon Ann," Julianne said, putting a hand on my back and steadying me.

Sharon Ann held her hands up, like her question was completely justified and Julianne was snapping at her for no reason.

I pulled my hand back from around my head and was relieved that my fingers were absent of blood. "What happened?"

Julianne stared intently at me, concern shaping her entire face. "We were on the phone. I saw someone behind you. You didn't. Whoever it was hit you with something. I saw it come up as you turned around, but I couldn't see what it was. Then you went down."

I kept running my fingers over the lump on the back of my head, the throbbing inside my skull growing stronger by the second. I thought I remembered the phone call and then falling to the pavement, but it was hazy.

Sirens screeched into the parking lot, and a loud murmur went up near the stairs. I looked over and realized that everyone that had come to see my fight with the WORMS was now staring at me on the sidewalk. Maybe I'd get the sympathy vote.

Two people at the edge of the crowd caught my eye. They were whispering to one another, nodding.

Shayna and Billy.

Was she violating her own restraining order by being there? Was that even allowed?

I tried to stand up, but waves of nausea crashed over me and my knee buckled before I could get to my feet. Dizziness swam around me, as if someone had wrapped me up in a big blanket and then spun me out of it.

"Easy," Julianne said, moving her hand to my shoulder, gently keeping me in a sitting position. "Paramedics are here. Just relax."

Darlene put her hand on my other shoulder. "I offered to give you CPR." She frowned at Julianne, her make-up giving her the look of a pissed-off clown. "But Julianne claimed you were breathing."

"Since you're awake now," Sharon Ann said,

glancing around, "maybe we can just hold the meeting out here. Shouldn't take long."

"Sharon Ann," Julianne said, standing up as the paramedics came to my side. "There will be no damn meeting tonight. And if you mention it again, you'll be the one riding away in the ambulance."

Sharon Ann's eyes narrowed, but she wisely took several steps away from us.

The two male paramedics began peppering me with questions, and I did my best to answer.

Yes, my head hurt like hell. No, I didn't know what I was struck with. Yes, I knew my name. No, I didn't have a history of head injuries. Yes, I felt like I wanted to vomit.

"He probably smells Sharon Ann," Julianne muttered, still shooting lasers out of her eyes at the woman.

"We should take you in for observation," the one paramedic said. "Think you've got a concussion."

I nodded slowly, my head feeling like a cement bowling ball. Normally, I would've resisted a trip to the hospital with every ounce of male ego I possessed. But my head hurt, and I knew I wasn't right.

"Can you stand?" he asked me.

I took a deep breath, trying to get everything around me to settle. "Think so."

The paramedic helped me to my feet. The world tilted to the right, and I started to list in that direction. He kept a tight grip on my elbow and pulled me back toward him. The school and the crowd righted themselves as my equilibrium found itself.

Shayna and Billy were walking away, toward the other side of the lot. Had they come just in hopes of seeing me get ousted? Or did one of them club me over the head?

"You all right?" the paramedic asked. "We can wheel you over."

I'd already conceded a hospital visit. I wasn't jumping on a gurney for a free ride. "I'm okay. Just hang on to me."

Julianne came up on my other side. "You want me to ride with you?"

"No, I'll be fine. Just drive over and meet us there."

She glanced back over her shoulder. "All right. I'm going to set everyone straight before I go, though."

We reached the back of the ambulance. I rubbed my temples, hoping to force some of the radiating pain out. "How's that?"

She stared back at the crowd at the top of the stairs as the paramedic opened up the doors on the back of the ambulance.

"Jules?" I said.

Her lips puckered like she'd bitten into a lemon gone wrong as she tore her eyes from the crowd. "Don't you worry about it." She stood on her tiptoes and kissed me on the cheek. "I'll be there shortly."

The paramedic helped me up the short set of stairs into the back of the ambulance, his hands steadying me as I wobbled my way up. I was bent at the waist so as not to smack my head against the roof. I shuffled my feet around to say one last goodbye to Julianne.

But she was already walking across the lot like her shoes were on fire, closing the distance between her and Sharon Ann McCutcheon.

32

"I think your midget friend is out there," Julianne said.

We were in the exam room at the hospital. They'd already stuck me in the tube and run a CT scan, which showed that all the important parts were still working. The doctor ran a few more simple tests on me before diagnosing me with a minor concussion. He told me that I'd have a pretty good headache for a couple of days, but after a few days of taking it easy, I would be back to normal.

Julianne had just arrived, and now she was talking about midgets.

"What?" I asked, wondering if the concussion was worse than the doctor realized.

She glanced over her shoulder again, toward the waiting room, her expression somewhere between amused and confused. "Didn't you say that investigator guy was a midget?"

"Yeah."

"Unless Rose Petal is offering some sort of relocation incentives to small people, I think your guy is out in the waiting room," she said. She wrinkled her nose. "He really is little."

The throbbing began anew in my head as I finished buttoning up my shirt. I had no idea what Victor Anthony Doolittle might be doing at the hospital, but I doubted it was a coincidence.

I slid off the exam table and slung my tie and coat over my shoulder. "If he touches me, I swear to God, I'm going to hang him in a closet."

Julianne rolled her eyes and led the way out.

Victor Doolittle was paging through a magazine when we walked into the waiting room. He was wearing the fedora again, paired with a Hawaiian shirt and slacks. He glanced up, tossed the magazine aside, and wiggled himself out of the chair.

He pointed up at me with a stubby finger. "How's the noggin?"

"Fine," I said. "What are you doing here?"

His eyes moved from me to Julianne. He removed his fedora and smiled. "Aren't you going to introduce me to this beautiful woman?"

"No."

He bowed in her direction. "Victor Anthony Doolittle, ma'am. It's my pleasure."

She extended her hand, smiling. "Julianne Winters."

He took her hand and kissed it.

The nausea rose up again from my stomach.

He slowly released her hand. "Your husband is a lucky, lucky man."

"Why, thank you," Julianne said, grinning at me.

"If things should ever sour between you two—"

"Hey," I said, cutting him off. "Enough. What are you doing here?"

He pried his eyes from Julianne, glaring at me. "Maybe I'm here for a physical."

"That shouldn't take long."

Deep lines formed on his wide forehead. "They take a look at your man parts in there? Make sure everything's still working?"

"Let's go," I said, walking past him and nudging Julianne along. "See you never."

"Whoa, whoa, whoa," he said, following behind me like an annoying talking Chihuahua. "Take it easy, King Kong."

I ignored him and kept my hand at the small of Julianne's back as she kept trying to look behind me to get another look at him.

We pushed through the doors and stepped out into the thick, humid night air.

"I was there, you moron," Victor said.

"Where?" I called over my shoulder. "Oz?"

"Tonight," he said. "I was there when somebody tried to knock your block off."

Against every instinct, I stopped in my tracks. Julianne stopped as well, and we both turned around.

Victor shrugged his shoulders and held his little hands out, palms up. "But, hey, maybe you don't care about that. Maybe you don't care if I saw something." He gave me a smug smile. "Maybe you got it all taken care of, big fella."

I couldn't tell if he was bluffing. But the fact that I knew he'd been following me for some time made me think he was telling the truth.

"What did you see?" I asked.

He laughed, a volley of snorts followed by what sounded like a sob. "I saw you go down like a condemned building."

"You wanna feel what it's like to be under that building?" I asked, stepping toward him.

He jumped into his ridiculous karate stance again, chopping at the air. I was ready to give him a nice kung fu kick to the side of his fat head.

Julianne stepped between us, placing a hand on my chest and giving me a stern look, telling me to knock it off.

She turned to Victor. "Mr. Doolittle, it would be a great help to us if you would share what you saw."

He looked past her at me. "He comes at me, I'll have to hurt him."

"He won't come after you," she assured him. "Right, Deuce?"

"No," I said. "His karate has frightened me. I am frozen in my tracks. Eek."

Doolittle missed my sarcasm, threw his shoulders back, and lifted his chin. "That's more like it."

"What did you see?" Julianne repeated.

"A truck," he said. "I was parked at the far end of the lot, out near the street."

"You were following me again?" I asked.

"Doing my job," he said. "I watched you get out of the van, walk there to the front of the steps, speak to Ms. Andrews, then answer your cell phone."

He definitely wasn't bluffing.

"Did you see who was behind Deuce?" Julianne asked.

"No," Victor said. "I was observing from my car. You were closer than I was when you pulled into the lot."

"But you saw a truck?" Julianne said, pressing.

He nodded. "Yep. It left the lot on the far side

during all the commotion of everyone rushing to help your husband."

"You get a license plate?" I asked. "A description of the truck?"

"Maybe."

My headache was threatening to blow my skull wide open, and my tiny little nemesis wasn't helping.

"Let's go, Jules," I said. "I don't care what Mighty Mouse says he saw."

His face fired up again, and his hands closed into fists. "Mighty Mouse? I'll stick my foot so far up your . . ."

Julianne reached out and touched him on the arm. "Please. Mr. Doolittle. Ignore him. He has a concussion. If you saw anything, we'd like to know."

He looked down at her hand on his arm, and his entire demeanor changed, like she was some sort of faith healer with a touch of the power. Her touch made him happy.

It infuriated me.

"I got a partial on the plate," he told her. "But I don't give information out for free. I'm an investigator, and I have to make a living."

"Jules, seriously," I said, ready to blow my top. "Screw Dopey. Let's go."

She held a rigid finger up in my direction.

"Mr. Doolittle," she said. "I'm sure that being an investigator, you'd hate to obstruct justice."

His smug expression weakened.

"And if you have information that might be helpful in solving tonight's assault, you would be guilty of just that," she explained. She smiled at him. "But I know you know that. So, please."

He thought about that for a moment, his eyes

shooting back and forth between me and Julianne. I wanted to poke his little beady eyes right out of his head.

Finally, his gaze settled on Julianne. "Lemme work on it. I'll come by your house tomorrow evening and tell you if I've got anything."

I started to object, but Julianne stopped me with her finger again.

"That'll be fine," Julianne told him. "We'll see you then."

"You bet you will, doll," he said, adjusting his fedora and backpedaling toward the parking lot. "Good luck getting me out of your dreams tonight, baby. This pretty face is hard to forget." He shot her with his forefinger. "Later."

Julianne hooked her arm with mine, and we started walking slowly toward the car.

"Do we have to serve him dinner?" I asked.

"That would be the polite thing to do."

"It'll be a tough decision, then."

She took out her keys as we reached the car. "What'll be a tough decision?"

"On what to serve," I said. "Short ribs or shrimp?"

33

When you have a concussion, even though the only thing you want to do is sleep, it is the last thing you are allowed to do. Some elected member of your family must wake you up every two hours in order to ensure that you haven't died, that your eyes still work, and that you still can't remember the date of your wedding anniversary.

So it was a long night.

I woke up for good around seven, as Julianne was dressing for work. My head felt as if someone had taken a large hammer and repeatedly struck me in the back of the head with it. The knot on my skull had grown from a small egg to a larger one.

I pushed myself to a sitting position. The nausea I'd experienced before was gone. My mouth was dry and my neck was sore and the headache was front and center, but I was okay.

Julianne emerged from the bathroom, working an earring into her lobe. "How are you?"

"Awesome."

"I already talked to your mother," she said,

smoothing the cream-colored skirt and jacket she had on. "She'll take care of Carly today."

Rather than bringing her home amid all the chaos, we'd let her spend the night with my parents.

I threw my legs over the side of the bed and stood up. My balance was back. I pulled on a T-shirt and followed Julianne out to the kitchen.

"You never told me what happened after I left in the ambulance," I said.

"Nothing, really."

"Nothing as in nothing, or nothing as in you punched Sharon Ann?"

She smiled. "Trust me. If I'd socked Sharon Ann, I'd be telling you."

"So what happened?"

She rifled through a stack of papers on the kitchen table. "I just told her to back off. And that if she insisted on going ahead with her little emergency meeting, she could expect a fight." She set the papers in a neat stack. "I may have called her a name or two, as well."

"Even with this headache, I've never found you more attractive," I said.

"I love it when a man with a brain injury flirts with me."

I went to the fridge and pulled out a carton of orange juice. "There was something I didn't get a chance to tell you yesterday."

Julianne's face wrinkled up with irritation. "Deuce, I swear, if you tell me you went and bought her a dog . . ."

Carly had been hounding us for months about wanting a dog. I was okay with it; Julianne was not.

She believed animals were meant to roam free. In Africa. Far away from her.

"Relax," I said, holding my hand up. "I don't have that kind of a death wish."

She watched me, not entirely sure I was telling the truth. I made a mental note to call the pet store and get my deposit back.

"I got some information on swimming lessons," I said.

Her features softened. "Oh. Good. Where?"

I stared into my glass of juice. "Tough Tykes."

I took a sip from the juice. At first, there was no initial furor, and I thought maybe I'd get away with it.

But I should've known better.

She bit the tip of her tongue for a moment before lashing me with it. "I know that you don't mean the same Tough Tykes that Benny supposedly went to before he died. Because if that was that specific Tough Tykes that you meant, you'd know how much I would disapprove and how my disapproval would lead to a stomach punch for you."

"I didn't say a word about Benny," I said, setting the juice down on the counter in case I had to block her punches. "I went in for swimming lesson info. That was it."

"Do I look stupid to you?"

"No. You look hot. Really hot. Like always."

"Deuce," she said, taking a deep breath, unswayed by my blatant sucking up. "You said you'd stay out of Benny's death."

"How does getting swim lesson information for our daughter have anything to do with Benny?" I pleaded. "Where else should I have gone?"

She didn't have an answer for that.

"The swimming pool looked great, and so do the lesson programs," I continued so she couldn't cut me off. "And Carly loved the place. I swear to you that I did not say one word to anyone about Benny. No questions, no comments, no nothing."

She studied me like a beautiful human polygraph machine, trying to decipher my blather. If I'd been lying, I would've wilted. But since, technically, I was telling the truth, I stood strong.

"Okay," she said.

"But that's not why I brought it up," I said.

"You are just killing me this morning, husband."

"I know. Sorry. But the guy that owns the place offered me a job."

Confusion spread across her face. "A job? What? Cleaning the pool?"

"Funny. No. Coaching football at their summer camps."

She grabbed the stack of papers off the table and slid them into her leather briefcase. "How exactly would that work?"

"I don't know."

She zipped the bag shut and looked at me. "Why are you telling me this?"

I shuffled my feet and bit the inside of my cheek. "Because I think I want to do it."

Actually, I knew I wanted to do it. I knew it the second he offered me the position. It wasn't that I didn't love being home with Carly. I did, and there was no doubt that she was still my first priority. But when he said he'd work with me on scheduling and let me call the shots, I was already thinking what the first day would be like.

"What about Carly?" Julianne asked, slipping the bag onto her shoulder. "What do we do with her? The whole reason you left the school was so that we wouldn't have to put her in day care or hire a babysitter."

"This wouldn't be like a full-time job, Jules," I said, frustrated that she wasn't immediately agreeing with me. "Couple of weeks during the summer. I can set the schedule any way I want so it works best for me. Shoot, I might be able to bring her with me."

"And fit her with a helmet and shoulder pads, probably."

"Couldn't hurt. She needs to work on her tackling."

She frowned.

"I'm kidding, Jules," I said. "About putting a uniform on her. But if we could figure it out, I think I'd like to do it."

She adjusted the bag and swiped her car keys off the table. "I've already got three cases on the calendar for the summer, plus our vacation. I don't have any wiggle room."

"I'm not asking you for any," I said. "If I can't make it work, I won't do it."

She shook her head, clearly not in favor of the idea. "I've gotta get going." She kissed me on the cheek. "I can't think on this right now. Let's talk about it tonight. When your head is better and you can see that this probably isn't a great idea."

34

I was given strict orders to lie around and relax.

So I ate some toast and took a hot shower and got dressed slowly.

Enough relaxing for me.

I drove over to Delilah's to join my father and his pals for breakfast, more because I had a few questions than because I was hungry. He, Cedric, Sheldon, and Judge Gerald Kantner were at their usual table.

My dad studied me as I approached them. "You look fine to me."

"A little uglier," Cedric said.

"Nah, he was always ugly," Sheldon said.

Gerald laughed into his coffee.

I grabbed a chair at the table across from them and slid it over next to Cedric. "Seriously. You guys are a riot. When I put you all in the old folks' home, you'll be the life of the place."

"Big words from a guy who fainted before his big confrontation with a bunch of mothers," Sheldon said, adjusting his glasses.

"I didn't faint. Somebody hit me."

Sheldon peered over the top of his glasses. "I know. It's just funnier when I tell people you fainted. Getting assaulted makes it sound like you're some sort of tough guy."

"Tough guy who doesn't check behind him," my father said.

"Maybe you got hit with a purse," Cedric suggested, then bit into some crisp bacon. "Someone with a heavy wallet. Maybe there was a make-up bag inside."

"Easy, gentlemen," Gerald Kantner said. "Deuce has had a rough couple of days."

Judge Gerald Kantner was the reasonable one in my father's quartet of pals. Short, thin, with a thick mop of dark hair on his head, he carried with him the serious presence you'd expect in a judge. He was always polite, always thoughtful, and always the one people looked to when they needed the right answer.

What he was doing with Huey, Dewey, and Louie, I wasn't sure.

"Judge," I said, offering my hand. "Haven't seen you in a while."

We shook, and he looked me right in the eye. "Sorry about the TRO, Deuce. Not much I could do, though."

"It's all right, Judge."

"TROs are strange nuts. You can obtain one almost without cause," he explained. "Someone comes in asking for one, it's awfully difficult to deny."

"So I could get one against any of these three?" I asked, pointing a finger at the other three men.

"I'll grant those right now, if you'd like."

They all rolled their eyes and continued eating.

I waved at Doris, the waitress, signaling for coffee, and she acknowledged me with a disinterested nod.

"Can I ask what the reasoning was?" I asked Gerald. "For the restraining order. Did she give a specific reason?"

The judge shook his head. "No. And she didn't appear. Billy handled the request."

That didn't surprise me. He seemed to be handling everything for her.

"He requested the order based on your visit," he said, folding up his napkin and laying it next to his plate. "Said you showed up uninvited, wouldn't leave, and that because she was under duress due to Benny's death, she did not want you returning."

"She called me," I said.

He raised an eyebrow. "Not the story I received."

I pulled out my cell and scrolled through the received calls log. I didn't see Shayna's name, and it puzzled me at first. Then I saw the word *Restricted.*

"The call came in restricted," I said. "But that was her."

The judge's lips twisted a bit, skepticism taking root. "As someone who's known you your entire life, I believe you. As an officer of the court, I'd need more than that."

My father stuck a fork in my direction. "She got you again, you big dope."

"Again?"

He set his fork down on the edge of his plate, wiped his mouth, and gave me that look that made me feel like I was ten years old and had screwed something up.

"Deuce, she was a pain in the ass when you pined for her in high school," he said. "She used you then, and she's using you now. Back then, I knew why. Because you were a star and she liked being along for the ride and she thought that ride was taking her all the way to the top. When the ride came to a screeching halt, she nearly broke her ankles jumping off so fast." His lips puckered like his eggs were filled with lemons. "This time, I don't know why, and I don't know what she's doing. But you can bet your ass she knew exactly what she was doing when she called you. Shayna has always been trouble in a pretty face."

The men fell quiet, the other sounds of the restaurant—dishes clanking, silverware clinking, and soft conversation—filtering across the table. My father wasn't stating anything I didn't already know, but he had a way of saying things that bit into me. He knew it and I knew it and it had been that way for as long as I could remember.

"Ah, take it easy on him, Eldrick," Sheldon said, lifting his coffee cup to his lips. "Shoot, can't blame the kid for wanting to see what was under her shirt." He paused, a wry smile spreading across his face. "Far as I've ever been able to tell, Shayna is blessed in that regard."

The laughter cut through the tension at the table. But my father was correct. She'd used me then, and she was using me now. I just didn't know why or how.

The judge stood and put a hand on my shoulder. "You can find me anything on the phone records, give me a call."

"Will do."

He walked out of Delilah's, saying good-bye to half the diner on his way out.

"Call was on your cell?" Cedric asked.

I nodded.

"Okay. I know a guy who might be able to help."

"Who?"

"Doesn't matter," Cedric said, waving a hand in the air. "I'll see if he can come up with anything for you."

"How's your head?" my father asked.

"All right. Have a headache, but I'm fine."

"Julianne told your mother you were supposed to be home in bed," he said, but his tone was less sharp than before.

"Yeah, well, keep it quiet then, all right?"

"Your funeral. Do not upset my Julianne."

"Blah, blah, blah."

Sheldon leaned across the table, his eyes darting around before settling on me. "Deuce. Seriously. One question."

My father and Cedric smiled, knowing what was coming, apparently. I didn't.

"Okay," I said.

He leaned a little farther across his plate. "Shayna. How blessed *is* she?"

35

After breakfast I went home to actually rest. The erratic night of sleep and the headache were catching up with me, and I didn't want to pass out somewhere in the middle of town. So I spent the rest of the morning on the sofa, watching ESPN and generally feeling like a slug.

Julianne called at noon. "Hope you're better by tomorrow."

"Why's that?"

"Just got an e-mail. The WORMS have rescheduled your hearing for tomorrow night."

The headache pulsed some more at the thought of that. "Great."

"Yeah. I say we go in with your head all bandaged up, shoot for the sympathy vote."

"I'll think about that," I said, hitting mute on the television. "You know anything about phone records?"

"A little. Why?"

I told her about Shayna claiming I went to her house uninvited and the restricted call.

"Could be tough to track," she said. "Those restricted lines tend to be hidden pretty good behind privacy laws."

"Cedric said he knows somebody who might be able to unlock it," I told her.

"I'll ask the investigator we use here in the office. Or maybe I'll ask your little friend tonight."

I could tell she was smiling.

"How is your head?" she asked before I could pop off.

"I'm fine."

"I didn't mean to douse your fire this morning," she said.

"I know. Shouldn't have sprung it on you like that. I just didn't want to keep it from you."

"It's just something we have to think about."

"I know. I get it."

"I promise to be a little less melodramatic about it tonight."

"Always a plus."

"Not saying I'll approve. But I will listen."

"That's all I want."

"No, what you want is for me to be thrilled about you doing this," she corrected. "And I'm not sure that'll happen, regardless of what we decide. But I promise to listen."

She would. She tended to go off like a firecracker initially, her stubbornness getting the better of her, before she lapsed into a more reasonable version of herself. Unlike me, who was always calm and cool and collected and never flew off the handle about anything. I didn't mention that difference to her, though.

"And don't think I missed the fact that you talked to Cedric this morning," she said. "Hope you enjoyed your morning out."

Stubborn, but didn't miss a damn thing.

36

Victor Anthony Doolittle said, “Seriously. You give me any crap tonight and I’ll give you another concussion.”

He was standing outside the screen door. I’d spent the rest of the afternoon lounging around the house, and the headache had finally subsided. I’d done some laundry and vacuuming and arranged to pick up Carly in the morning. I didn’t want her to be traumatized by Victor.

I pushed open the door. “I promise to watch my step.”

He looked pleased with that, as if he’d actually scared me. “Good, because I’d hate to have to hurt . . .”

“I meant I’d try not to catch you under my shoe.”

The blood rushed to his face, and his face screwed up in anger.

“Relax,” I said. “I’m kidding. We invited you. I’ll be on my semi-best behavior.”

The anger slowly receded from his features, and

he glanced around the living room. "Where's your wife?"

"She'll be here shortly," I told him. "She's running late. You find anything out?"

He smiled at me, but he looked more like Grumpy than Happy. "Yes."

We stood there for a moment. It was clear he wasn't going any further.

"You want something to drink?" I finally asked.

"Mint julep."

"Try again."

"A Flaming Eyeball."

"I could find a cat to piss in a cup."

"Beer's fine."

I retreated to the kitchen and grabbed two Lone Stars out of the fridge. I felt certain that I wasn't supposed to drink with a concussion. But there was a sarcastic dwarf in my living room, and I needed something to take the edge off.

He was sitting on the sofa, his feet sticking off the end of the cushion and his fedora on his lap. I handed him the beer, and he made a face like I'd actually brought him the cat piss. "Lone Star? Really?"

"It's Julianne's favorite," I lied, sitting down in the chair across from him.

His expression immediately changed, the beer magically morphing into the greatest thing he'd ever seen. He took a long drink and wiped his mouth with the back of his hand. "So."

"So."

"We havin' dinner?"

"Julianne's bringing food home."

"Excellent."

"And if you want to eat any of it, let's hear what you found out."

He took another drink and moved the fedora from his lap to the arm of the sofa. "I can find out who owns the truck."

"You got the full license plate?"

He nodded. "I started with the partial and worked my way through it. I've got friends at TxDOT."

I didn't think he had friends anywhere, but I let it go.

He reached into his pocket and pulled out a piece of paper. "Truck was a Ford Ranger."

"Any way to find out who owns it?"

He rolled his eyes like I'd asked him if he knew how to spell his own name. "Of course. There is always a way to find anything out." He tapped his forehead with the beer bottle. "If you're smart. Which, lucky for you, I am."

I was being talked down to by an arrogant midget. Where had I gone wrong?

The front door opened and Julianne walked in, several bags smelling of barbecue in her arms.

Victor wiggled off the sofa and ran to her knee, reaching up with his hands. "Let me help."

"Oh, thank you, Victor," she said, handing him one of the bags. "That's kind of you."

He beamed. "My pleasure. A lady shouldn't have to do all the work around here." He tossed me a dirty look.

We organized ourselves around the kitchen table, spreading out the brisket sandwiches and baked potatoes. Julianne did a quick change into a pair of jeans and a T-shirt and sat down next to me, across from Victor, who was halfway through one sandwich already.

"What did I miss?" she asked.

"Victor was about to tell me who owns the truck he saw in the parking lot," I said.

He dabbed at the corners of his mouth with a napkin. "Yes, ma'am. I did my due diligence and was able to locate the pickup truck that I saw at the scene of your husband's assault." He frowned. "He hasn't yet thanked me for that, though."

I started to say something, but Julianne clasped a hand onto my thigh. "He has a concussion. He's not thinking correctly. I'm sure he meant to thank you."

He wolfed down the rest of the first sandwich and grabbed for another. "Sure, sure. Okay." He pulled the piece of paper from before out of his lap and laid it on the table. "Owner's name is Zeke Stenner."

The name meant nothing to me.

"Did you do any checking on him?" I asked.

He wrinkled his nose at me. "No."

"Why not?"

He bit into the sandwich and chewed with his mouth open for a moment. "Because you didn't hire me to."

My impulse was to reach across the table and smack the food right out of his fat little hand. Julianne could sense it, though, and dug her nails into my leg again.

"Of course we didn't," she said. "We appreciate you tracking the license plate, though."

"Anything for you, sweetheart."

"That's all we get?" I asked, unable to contain myself. "We let you come over here, feed your fat face, and that's all we get?"

The barbecue sauce was smeared all over his mouth now as he laughed. “Hey. I didn’t say you had to feed me. And you didn’t hire me. I did what I did as a courtesy. You want more, it’s gonna cost you.”

Julianne looked at me. “It’s all right, Deuce. I spoke to the investigator at our firm. He owes me a favor.”

The smug smile on Victor’s face evaporated.

“Excellent,” I said, looking at him and grinning.

“Whoa, whoa, whoa,” he said, holding up his sauce-covered palm. “Let’s hold on a sec here. I didn’t say we couldn’t work something out.”

Julianne fluttered her eyes at him. “Oh? Really?”

“For a nominal fee, I’m sure we can work together.”

“Define *nominal fee,*” I said.

“How about if we discuss it after you get me another beer?” he said.

Before I could dunk his head in the barbecue sauce, Julianne had the good sense to claw my leg one more time.

“That sounds like a good idea,” she said, smiling at me. “And will you grab me one, too? But I’d like a Shiner Blonde. You know I can’t stand that Lone Star stuff.”

Victor glared at me.

I had to admit, it was fun tricking dwarves.

37

After another beer and another brisket sandwich, Victor Anthony Doolittle said, "Three hundred bucks will get it done."

Julianne turned to me. "The investigator at my office? I set up a trust for his mother, who has cancer. He was so grateful—"

"Two hundred," Victor said, wiping a paper napkin across his face. "Half up front, the other half when I get you a full write-up on this Stenner guy."

"One fifty," I said. "Payable as you said."

His lips tightened up, and the skin on his bald head stretched tighter across his skull.

Julianne just batted her eyelashes some more.

"Deal," he said.

I wrote him a check for seventy-five bucks, and we escorted him to the door.

"I'll call you tomorrow," he said, staring at Julianne.

She pointed at me. "Call him."

The corners of his mouth turned downward, as

if she'd asked him to eat something out of a trash can. "Fine."

The phone rang, and Julianne excused herself to go answer it.

I walked out with Victor. It was strange. In twenty-four hours, I'd gone from taking a shot in the groin from him to hiring him. It felt like we'd known each other for far too long.

He walked over to bright red convertible MG parked at the curb.

"That's yours?" I asked.

He nodded. "Yep. Chick magnet."

"Not what you were driving yesterday."

"Man, you tall guys are mentally deficient," he said, shaking his head as he opened the door to the sports car. "I was following you. It was a rental. This is *my* car."

"You ever plan on telling me why you were following me?" I asked. "Who was running some background check on me?"

He removed the fedora and tossed it like a Frisbee onto the passenger seat. "Look, I know you're curious. But part of what I get paid for is to keep my mouth shut." He held a stubby finger up. "For instance. When I run down whoever Stenner is—and I will run him down—if he and I get face-to-face, he's gonna wanna know who hired me." He pointed the stubby finger at me. "Even though I just gave you and your unbelievably stunning wife a sweet deal, it's still a deal. That guy won't get your name from me, I promise you that. That's the way it works."

Cedric told me that he'd heard that Victor Anthony Doolittle was good at what he did. I didn't like him sneaking into my backyard, and I sure as hell didn't like him flirting with my wife, but until that moment I hadn't seen him as anything more than an arrogant little person. He was, in fact, a professional.

"Fair enough," I said.

"I know," he said, crawling into the seat of the MG.

I could see blocks on the pedals, and the driver's seat appeared to have been customized to his height.

He turned the key in the ignition, and the engine fired to life. He gunned it for a moment, letting it rev high.

He looked over his shoulder at me. "Tomorrow. I'll call you." A sneaky smile spread across his face. "And then I'll let your wife thank me."

I jumped at the car and it screeched away from the curb, his weird little snorty laugh echoing back at me as he drove away.

38

Julianne and I went to bed early, feeling tired and groggy from the staccato rhythm of the previous night's sleeping schedule. When I woke the next morning, my headache was gone and the lump on the back of my head seemed to be receding.

I drove over to my parents to pick up Carly and take her to school.

My mother had her dressed and sitting on the sofa, waiting for me, when I walked into their living room.

"How'd you do that?" I askcd.

"Do what?" my mother said.

"Get her to sit still."

My mother chuckled the laugh of a mother who knew all the tricks. "I just asked her."

"Can I go hug Daddy now?" Carly asked, already inching off the sofa.

"Of course," my mother and I said at the same time.

She bounced over to me, and I bent down so she could grab me around the neck. She clutched onto me like I'd been gone for six months, her damp hair cold against my cheek. I would face a thousand Doolittles, Caldwells, and WORMS for one of those hugs any day.

She pulled back, her pink lips pursed together tightly in concern. "Grandma said you hit your head."

"I did, but I'm okay now."

"Papa said there wasn't anything in your head to hurt," she stated. "Is that true? Is your head empty?"

My mother shook her head and let out a disgusted sigh.

"My head is just fine," I said. "Papa is the one with the empty head."

"Deuce. Don't encourage it."

"We're all fine," I told Carly before she could ask more questions about her grandfather's faculties.

My mother followed us out to the minivan. "Buckle her in. Wanna share something with you, Deuce."

I got Carly situated in her car seat, shut the door, and turned to face my mother.

"I heard something yesterday," she said, waving at Carly on the other side of the window. "I took Carly over to the park and ran into some of the ladies."

Some of the ladies could have meant just about anyone, as my mother was probably better known throughout Rose Petal than I was. She'd never held a job her entire life, but she'd spent every free moment volunteering on just about every committee she could possibly find. As a result, if there was a lady she didn't know, it was either because she was new to town or she'd just been born. She used the phrase "the ladies" to simplify the process of telling a story, because if she had to stop and explain to me who specifically she was speaking about every time she referred to a female friend, we'd never get to the point in the conversation.

"They, of course, wanted to know what the story was with you," she said, moving her eyes from the van to me. "I set them straight, that none of this was your doing."

"Thanks."

"I would've lied if needed."

"Uh. Thanks again?"

"Anyway," she said, folding her arms across her chest, "there was some scuttlebutt about Shayna."

"When isn't there scuttlebutt about Shayna?"

"Well, I thought once you found the good sense to break up with that girl, we would've been free of the scuttlebutt."

"Mom, she broke up with me. And it was twenty years ago."

She rolled her eyes. "And, yet, it still hangs around our necks like an albatross we can't get rid of."

While my father tolerated Shayna when we dated, my mother would just stare at her, attempting to turn her into dust. She never bought into the whole glamorous couple of Rose Petal High idea. Shayna rubbed her the wrong way from the first day she met her, and that enmity had only grown over time.

When Shayna broke up with me, my mother told everyone that I broke up with her. She just couldn't stand the idea that her son had been dumb enough to not get out of a relationship with Shayna first.

"Anyway," she said, brushing the truth aside, like always. "There was some discussion about Shayna."

"Why would I care about this, Mom?"

She glanced in the window and wrinkled her nose at Carly, who giggled inside. "Because it would appear that Ms. Barnes wasn't exactly faithful to her husband. I know that's about as surprising as finding out that water is wet, but there it is."

I thought of Odell Barnabas's insinuations and nodded. "I heard that, too. Nothing concrete, though."

My mother cocked an eyebrow. "Well, Lillian Vardan saw something concrete."

"Lillian Vardan has glasses thicker than a bank vault."

"Watch your mouth," she said, pointing a finger at me. "She saw them over in McLinney several weeks back. Some Italian restaurant. In a booth, where they could paw at each other."

The thought of Shayna pawing at Odell's hair was somewhere between laughable and disgusting. I didn't get it, but I didn't want to think about it anymore.

"Mom, I don't need the details on this," I said, squeezing the car keys. I kissed her on the cheek. "I could care less what she and Odell do."

She pulled back, her eyes narrowed and her lips pressed together. "Who is Odell?"

"The guy," I said. "With the big, fake hair. Who may or may not have been having an affair with Shayna Barnes."

"I have no idea who the man with big, fake hair is."

The headache was returning at breakneck speed. "I thought you just said Lillian saw Shayna and Odell over in McLinney. I already heard that maybe she had something going with him."

"Lillian did see her over in McLinney," my mother said. "But not with someone named Odell."

"Then who was she with?"

My mother smiled triumphantly. "She had her mouth all over Billy Caldwell."

39

The image of Billy's mouth all over Shayna creeped me out the entire drive to Carly's school.

It wasn't that I thought either of them was above having an affair. In fact, they both seemed exactly the type. While I thought Odell's remarks about sleeping with her were a bit odd and I would never see why anyone would be attracted to Odell, never for a moment did I think he was lying.

And Billy was just the sort of guy to overlook a marriage license when pursuing a woman.

I just hadn't figured that they would be doing it together.

So to speak.

As I unbelted Carly and helped her jump out of the van, I tried to expunge the image from my head.

Carly skipped all the way to the front door of her classroom. I hoped she would feel the same way about school when she was sixteen, but knew that was wishful thinking.

Sally Meadows sidled up to me as I signed Carly in. "How are you?"

"I'm fine."

"Are you ready for tonight?"

I set the pen down on the clipboard. "As ready as I'm getting, I guess."

"Those women are frothing, waiting to get at you. Just keep your wits about you and you'll be fine." She swept her eyes over the classroom to make sure no one was in a headlock. "I've been putting the good word out for you. You'll have some support in the room."

"Thanks, Sally. I appreciate it."

"Just try not to get knocked out tonight." She made a beeline for a little boy who was about to snack on some finger paint.

I stepped out of the room and nearly knocked over Detective Willie Bell.

He puffed out his chest. "Mr. Winters."

"Detective."

"Wanted to ask you about the other night."

"I answered questions for one of your guys at the hospital."

He nodded. "Yes, sir. Just wanted to get my own take."

I moved over to the window. Carly was jabbering in another little girl's ear. "Okay."

"See anything?"

"No. Got hit from behind."

"Hear anything?"

"Yes. My wife on the cell phone, telling me to look out."

"So she saw something?"

Carly and the girl she was talking to dissolved into laughter. "Not really. It was dark."

He stood next to me at the window, his posture

ramrod straight and his eyes solely on me. He was like a dorky robot.

"Wanna know what I think?" he asked.

"Not particularly."

"I think you're making it up."

I let his words burn slowly through my head. It shouldn't have surprised me or made me angry. But it did both.

I turned to him. "You what?"

"I think you made it up," he said, smiling like he knew something I didn't.

"You're insane," I said.

"Staged the whole thing," he said. "You were even smart enough to have your wife call so there'd be a record of the conversation."

"And then what? I took a bat to my own head?"

"Maybe you didn't even get hit," he suggested, shoving out his bottom lip. "Not hard to fake a concussion."

I turned and pointed to the lump on the back of my head. "What do you think that is? A tumor?"

I whipped back around. I knew the lump was clearly visible. For a moment, his resolve wavered.

Not for long, though. "Maybe your wife hit you. If she made the call, she was already in on it."

Carly and the other girl were now chasing each other, their hands covered in paint. Sally was attempting to corral them.

"And tell me exactly why I would allow my wife to take a swing at me," I said. "Because I'm missing that part."

"You didn't wanna go to your big meeting last night," Bell said. "You knew that you were going to lose your position, and you thought you'd postpone the proceedings, maybe make people feel a little sorry for you." He folded his arms across his chest. "You can run, Winters, but you can't hide."

"That makes no sense," I said. "If you're gonna speak in clichés, at least use ones that fit the bull your spewing."

Pink splotches blossomed across his forehead. "You know what I mean."

The door to the classroom swung open, and Carly and the other girl charged out, screaming with glee, their painted hands up in the air. Sally spilled out into the hallway behind them. "Girls!"

"Daddy!" Carly said, making a beeline right for me, her palms up.

Her pal followed right on her footsteps.

I stepped to the side and caught Carly around the waist before she could plant her hands on me. The other little girl had no one to stop her, and she planted her hands on the first thing she ran into.

Detective Willie Bell's pants.

Two bright purple handprints right on his groin.

Their screaming died off immediately, the way it does when kids know something has gone awry and punishment may follow. Sally covered her mouth, her expression a mix of consternation and amusement. Detective Bell looked down at the fresh coat of paint on his pants, the pink splotches growing on his face by the second.

I smiled at Carly's friend. "And who are you?"

She tucked her chin down to her chest, a shy grin on her face. "Charlotte."

"Her name is Charlotte, Daddy," Carly reiterated, in case I missed it the first time around.

"Charlotte, I think you and I are gonna be friends," I told her.

She giggled.

"Girls, let's go back in our room and clean up," Sally said, taking each of them by the wrist. She looked at Bell. "I'm very sorry." She herded the little artists back inside her classroom.

Bell's face was turning into a tomato as he looked from his pants to me and back to his pants.

"You know what I think?" I asked him.

"What?" he said between clenched teeth.

"Purple on you," I said, pretending to think about it. "Purple on you is just nuts."

40

Victor Anthony Doolittle was pacing between his MG and my minivan when I stepped out into the parking lot.

He looked up as I approached, his forehead wrinkled in thought beneath the fedora. "What took you so long?"

"I was in there maybe fifteen minutes."

"Normally takes you seven."

I hated that he knew my life better than I did. "I didn't know we had an appointment this morning."

"We didn't." He rubbed his chin. "But something's come up, and I knew you'd be here."

Several cars drove past us, out of the lot. "Okay. What's up?"

He took the fedora off and scratched the top of his head. "Well, I'm not exactly sure."

I leaned against the van and let him work it out.

"See, things have kind of crossed paths," he finally said. "I did not anticipate that, and it's rare that I don't anticipate things."

"Do you anticipate me driving away if you don't start making sense?" I asked.

"I anticipate you staying right there and listening to me."

"Then quit talking like someone who just learned a bunch of new words."

He held his hands out, indicating that I needed to settle down. "Easy, Stilts."

I kept my mouth closed.

"I did some looking on our guy," he explained.

"Stenner?"

"Right."

"Found him."

"Great."

His nose twitched. I resisted the urge to make a rabbit joke.

"But some of what I found on Stenner . . ." His voice trailed off.

"Victor, you've got five seconds to spit it out or I'm outta here," I said, exasperated. "I've got things to do."

"Like what? Laundry?"

As a matter of fact.

"Stenner," he said. "He's a college kid. Twenty years old."

"All right."

"He teaches martial arts part-time," Victor said. "Lives over in Duncan. Just a kid."

I nodded, not that any of that made sense. We didn't know for certain that he was the guy that hit me. But why was some part-time karate guy flying out of the Rettler-Mott parking lot after I'd eaten the pavement?

"Okay," Victor said, holding up a short index finger. "I've made a decision."

"About what?"

"I'm gonna tell you something," he said. "But I need your word that it stays between us."

"You have it."

He held out his hand. "Shake on it. That way I'll know you mean it."

I shook his warm, clammy, action figure–like hand. "You have my word."

He glanced around, as if someone might be eavesdropping. I couldn't imagine anyone who'd want in on a conversation between a disgraced Room Dad and a dwarf private investigator.

"The guy who hired me," he said, convinced we were alone. "To do the background check on you? Guy named Jimmy Landry."

"The Tough Tykes guy?" I said.

"One and the same."

All along, I had just assumed it was Billy Caldwell that hired him. Hearing Landry's name really surprised me.

"Why?" I asked.

Victor shrugged. "Don't know. I don't ask why when I take a job. If it's something I do, then I just do it. Less I know, the better."

I expected a weird, shady vibe from Landry when I went to Tough Tykes, but ended up walking away impressed. Not just with the facility, but with him. He was nothing like I expected. So why was he interested enough in me to hire someone to check me out?

Which led to another question.

I looked at Victor. "Why are you telling me this? I thought it was against your code or something."

"It is against my code," he said. "Ethically, I'm doing the wrong thing by telling you this. Could ruin my reputation, if it gets out that I haven't protected a client's privacy."

"So why tell me?"

The corners of his mouth twitched, and he again scanned the lot before letting his eyes settle on me again. "Because this Zeke Stenner? He works for Landry."

41

"That's where he teaches martial arts," Victor said. "At Tough Tykes."

I watched the parade of minivans and SUVs continue out of the school parking lot.

"The kid also has a record."

"A record?"

"Nothing big," Victor said, waving his hand in the air. "But he was charged with a misdemeanor last year. Some sort of fight and assault."

"So it could've been him that hit me," I said.

"All of it sorta fits together," Victor said, nodding his head. "Him being here, you getting whacked, then him leaving."

It did sorta fit together.

"But when I was checking on him this morning and saw where he worked, it just didn't feel right," Victor said, sucking in his cheeks. "You know this Landry guy?"

"Barely," I said and explained my interaction with him.

Victor rubbed his chin. "He hired me before he spoke to you, then. What did you talk about?"

"Not much. He asked if I might be interested in a job. I didn't say no."

Victor shrugged. "Places like that do checks all the time on their employees. Working around kids, they gotta make sure you ain't all touchy-feely."

"But he hasn't hired me yet. For anything. And why would he hire you before he'd even spoken to me?"

Victor hunched his small shoulders again, telling me that was his best guess.

I tried to back up. "Wait. Let's go back to Stenner. Even if Landry hired you for the background check on me, why would one of his employees assault me?"

"I'm not saying he did," Victor said, holding up an index finger. "I'm just saying there's a connection and I thought it was weird. And I don't like weird."

Twenty-four hours ago I would've found a joke in that statement. But now it was starting to feel like Victor and I were on the same side.

"So what do we do?" I asked.

"We?" he asked, raising his eyebrows. "You got a pet rock in your pants? There is no we."

"Come on," I said.

"I'm serious," he said, shaking his head. "I told you this as a courtesy. I am not in your employ at the moment."

"The hell you aren't," I said. "We agreed on that last night."

"No, you agreed to hire me to find out about Stenner," he pointed out. "Which I've done. That was the deal. You want more than that, it's gonna cost you. Business is business."

I thought about that. The right thing to do would've been to call Julianne and let her know about Stenner and to discuss all of this in a reasonable, adult fashion.

But it wasn't like she was used to me doing the right thing.

"Fine," I said. "I wanna hire you. Again."

He fidgeted with the fedora. "Okay."

"On one condition."

He sighed. "And what's that?"

"We work together."

"Together? What are you talking about?"

"I want in," I said. "I wanna do a little investigating, too."

He held up his hands. "No way. I work solo."

"Cash up front," I said.

His hands wavered. "Up front?"

I nodded. Everything the last few days had been happening to me. I'd been reactive, and I was tired of it. It was time to start being proactive.

"Look," I said. "I just wanna figure this out, okay? I won't get in your way. But I can help."

He eyes were heavy with doubt. "How's that?"

I grinned at him. "I've got a plan."

42

I turned onto the access road that fed into the parking lot in front of Tough Tykes.

Victor leaned forward in the passenger seat, smashed his hands against the dash of the minivan. "What are you doing?"

"I told you. I had a plan."

"This is your plan? I told you, Winters. Landry can't know that I've talked to you. You promised!"

"Keep your short little pants on," I said, turning into the lot and gliding into a slot at the far end. "He's not going to know anything."

Beads of sweat formed on his wrinkled forehead. "So what exactly is your plan?"

"I'm going to test him," I said.

"Test who? Landry?"

"Yep."

He unbuckled the seat belt. "That's it. I'm out. You screwed me." He dropped to the floorboard and grabbed on to the door handle.

I reached out and grabbed the back of his jacket. "Hold on, hold on."

"Let go of me," he said, swatting at me with his hand. "I'm getting out of here."

"I'm going in," I said. "You're not."

He stopped swatting. "This may be the worst plan ever."

I wasn't in a position to disagree yet. But it was the only plan that came to mind, and I thought it was safe.

"We shook hands," I said. "It meant we had a deal. And I intend to honor that."

He twisted around so his back was against the door, his eyes suspicious.

"Just wait here," I said. "You can get in the back and get down. No one will see you. This'll just take a couple of minutes."

"What are you going to do?"

"Just trust me," I said, opening my door. "And get in the back. I think there's some goldfish back there if you get hungry."

He showed me his middle finger as I shut the door.

The front desk was staffed by a different perky girl this time. Her name tag said her name was Melanie.

"Hi, Melanie," I said, all smiles and daisies. "Is Jimmy around?"

She showed me her gleaming white teeth. "Do you have an appointment?"

"I don't. But could you just tell him Deuce Winters is here?"

She shrugged and disappeared down the back hallway.

As I stood there, the nerves started to infiltrate my cool and collected exterior. I was out of my element. I was acting on behalf of too many television shows and movies I'd watched over the years. If there really was something tying Landry to my taking a shot to the head, then I was about to set the bar unbelievably high for acts of stupidity.

Before I could turn tail and sprint out of there, Melanie was back, grinning at me.

"Mr. Landry says to go on back," she said, lightning bolts of enthusiasm shooting out of her expression. "He'd love to see you."

I didn't know whether that was a good thing or a bad thing.

43

Jimmy Z. Landry was out from behind his desk, wearing a brilliant red golf shirt and khaki shorts that appeared to have never seen a wrinkle in their lifetime.

"Deuce," he said, his hand extended. "Good to see you again."

We shook.

"I hope I'm not barging in on you," I said, half wishing he would say that I was and I could do a U-turn right out of his office.

"Not a chance," he said, gesturing at the chair I'd sat in previously. "Have a seat."

We both sat.

I cleared my throat. "So I wanted to talk to you a little more about the coaching thing."

He gave me a don't-tease-me smile. "You serious?"

"I am."

"I wasn't sure whether you'd have any interest," he said, smiling. "Thought we might be a little under your radar."

"Under my radar?"

"You know, too small-time. I know you're used to big-time football and coaching high school ball." He tapped his fingers on his desk. "This won't be nearly as exciting. You'll get a lot of kids who aren't good athletes, probably won't even make a JV team when they get to high school."

"I don't care," I said.

"Not that I'd want you to treat them any differently," he said, the smile thinning. "One of the things that we do here is make kids feel like they belong. They don't get teased here if they can't catch a ball or throw a spiral. It's our job to show them how to do those things, regardless of what their ability is or how competitively they are going to try and play. Kids should walk out of here feeling better about themselves."

In my head, I kept vacillating.

Shtick or sincere?

"So I'd want you to take these kids and make them feel like football players, not like players who are never going to make a team." He leaned back in his chair, his gaze firmly set on me. "That sound like something that would interest you?"

"It does," I said. "I've had my share of football under a microscope. In a lot of ways, I think this might be more fun."

He nodded. "That's what I'm looking for."

"Then I think I'm interested," I said. "Provided you can be flexible with scheduling."

"We've got three weeks until we need to get the camp brochures out in public," he said, the smile strengthening again. "You tell me what works for you and how you wanna do it and we'll make it happen."

"Sounds great."

He rubbed his hands together like they were cold. "Now. Here's the part that's not so great. I make a promise to everyone that works for me that they'll all be treated the same. I know you bring a bigger presence here, but I can't pay you for that. You'd be paid just like any other staff member working their first camp."

"I'm not gonna get rich?"

He chuckled. "Not a chance. Biggest perks I can give you are letting you set the schedule and giving you a free shirt. And maybe we can set something up to keep your daughter busy while you're here. Live with that?"

"No problem," I said, realizing I wanted the job, but I still wasn't getting anywhere. "Do we need to do some sort of application process?"

He produced a folder from his desk. "Some typical forms that I'll need back from you as soon as you can get them done. And we do a background check on everyone that is employed here." He held out a small index card. "You'll need to be fingerprinted, too. All the information you need is here." He dropped the card back into the folder and slid it across the desk to me.

"What kind of background check do you do?" I asked, my words sounding rushed and slurred.

He pursed his lips and tapped them with his fingertips. "I'm more thorough than most. We do the state-mandated one, and then I do my own. Two layers." He made a fist and knocked it on his desk.

"To protect the kids and let parents know that that's my first concern."

I took the folder. "Sure. Great."

"And to be up front," he said, looking not the least bit hesitant, "I've already started the process on you."

I tried to look surprised. "The process?"

"Generally, it takes close to three weeks for me to get back what I want to get back on any employee," he explained. "I use an investigative agency, and that's the window of time they need to complete the check."

"But you haven't hired me yet."

"No, but on the off chance you were interested, I wanted to get the ball rolling," he said, knocking his fist against the desk again. "With the summer deadlines rolling in, I wanted to be ready in case you were interested." He held up his palms in an apologetic fashion. "So I actually talked to my guy before you and I met. Wanted to make sure you were the good guy everyone said you were before I made an overture. You took me by surprise when you came in the other afternoon, but I felt like that was a sign that you were supposed to come work here. I hope you're not offended by that."

"No, no," I said quickly, standing. "That makes sense. And I don't have anything to hide."

He laughed loudly and rose on the other side of the desk. "I'm sure you don't." He extended his hand. "Deuce, I look forward to working with you."

As I shook his hand, the vacillating came to a halt.

I was certain that Jimmy Z. Landry was 100 percent sincere.

44

Victor was lying beneath the back bench in the minivan when I returned.

He stuck his head out from underneath, looking uncomfortable and anxious. "So?"

"So I'm not comfortable talking to anyone hiding beneath my daughter's car seat," I said, starting the van. "Get up here."

"No way," he said. "Not until we're long gone. Can't risk it."

"Victor, he admitted to the background check," I told him. "It's cool."

"Doesn't mean we should be cohorting together."

"I thought we were dating."

"Funny. But I don't date guys who look like Godzilla."

"But you do date guys?"

"What? No. I . . . Shut up."

I started the van, laughing at my own juvenile behavior. The doors to Tough Tykes opened, and a guy walked out.

"Hey, what does Stenner look like?" I asked.

"Medium build, crappy haircut, walks kind of funny. Why?"

I watched the kid crossing the lot. Medium build, a haircut straight from the Beatles era, and a long, loping stride.

"Sit up and look at this kid. To our left."

He grunted a couple of times, and I saw his head pop up slowly in the back, his eyes and nose barely cracking the bottom of the window. "Oh yeah. That's him. Walks like an ostrich or something, yeah?"

He did, in fact, walk like an ostrich.

"Get back down," I said, pulling out of the stall and heading left down the lot.

"What are you doing?" he asked, and I could tell from his voice that he was already back on the floor.

"Getting into this investigator thing," I said.

I cruised down the lot until I was behind Stenner.

I pushed the button, and my window slid down. "Excuse me."

Stenner slowed and glanced over his shoulder. "Yeah?"

"Is this Tough Tykes?"

He stopped and turned around, his eyes halfway through a roll. "Uh, yeah. Don't you see the sign?"

"Must've missed it," I said.

He stood, his slumped shoulders and lifted chin radiating annoyance. He was maybe twenty years old, medium height, and had a thin, lanky frame that didn't look at all intimidating in the way I imagined a martial arts instructor to be. A thin soul patch ran from his bottom lip to a rounded jaw. Eyes the color of mud stared at me, daring me to ask another question.

He raised his hand and pointed at the building.

"Front doors are right there. They can help you inside."

"You work here?" I asked.

He glanced down at his shirt with the Tough Tykes logo, then back at me.

Victor snorted from his hidden crouch in the back of the van.

Deuce Winters, Ace Investigator.

"Okay, thanks," I said.

Stenner shook his head, as if he wished he'd exited into another parking lot.

I eased the van out of the parking lot.

"What exactly were you doing?" Victor asked, ambling out from the back of the van to the front seat.

"Did you summon the courage to get a look out the window?" I asked. "Or were you just counting all the Gummy Bears on the floor?"

"I was maintaining a covert position," he said, buckling himself back into the seat.

I wanted to ask if he was supposed to be sitting in a car seat, but I thought that might be pushing it.

"I wanted to see his expression," I said.

"His expression?"

"When he saw me."

Victor thought it through, then nodded. "Got it. Actually, that's not bad."

"Thank you."

"Don't give yourself a hernia patting yourself on the back," Victor said, cutting his eyes to me. "If he was dangerous at all, he could've taken you out right there."

My stomach sank.

"I, of course, would've then saved you. Maybe."

"Gee, thanks."

Victor shifted in the seat, tugging at the belt near his neck. "So. His expression?"

"No clue," I said.

"No clue? You got that close and you have no clue?"

"No, bozo," I said to Victor as we drove. "Stenner had no clue who I was."

"You sure?"

Nothing registered in the kid's eyes other than contempt when he saw me. If he'd been the one to clock me in front of the school, I was certain that he would've reacted to my just showing up. Nervousness, anger, fear, something. He was either a master thespian or he had never seen me before.

"I'm sure," I said.

"Well, I know that he owns the truck," Victor said. "I ran it through the DMV."

"So, what? Coincidence then that he was there?"

Victor frowned at me. "Coincidences are for people who try to give pancakes to rats."

"That makes no sense."

He waved me off like I was mentally deficient. "Yes, it does. But it wasn't a coincidence, and it was Stenner's truck."

"So someone else was driving the truck, then?" I said.

Victor Anthony Doolittle clapped a couple of times in a blatant display of mockery. "Well done, Sherlock. Well done."

I tapped the brakes and he jerked forward, the belt catching him around the neck, gagging him for just a moment.

Made me feel better.

45

I returned Victor to the parking lot at school.

"I'll do some digging around today," he said, hopping into the MG. "See what I come up with." He threw his head back toward the school. "Have fun tonight. Try not to let the ladies embarrass you."

"Try not to get mistaken for a kindergartener," I said.

His laugh drifted into the air as he sped off.

It was time to stop goofing off and go to work.

I went home and threw some laundry in, did the dishes, and picked up around the house. I returned a movie to the video store and picked up Julianne's dry cleaning.

The important things.

I picked up Carly at school and dropped her off at my parents. There had been some thought on my part that taking her to the meeting might win me a little sympathy. But I figured it probably wasn't a good idea for her to be there, in case I started dropping profanity-laced rants on the WORMS.

My father was nowhere to be found, and my mother wished me a perfunctory "good luck."

"Don't get Carly kicked out of the school," she suggested. "I could care less about what happens to you, but don't go messing up that little girl's life."

It was funny how once grandchildren were born, children were dropped to the bottom of the parental food chain and the grandkids sat at the top. I could've been choking on a piece of food and the first thing that would've occurred to my mother would have been to move Carly out of the way so that when/if the food ever came out of my throat, it would not strike her in the face. If I fell over dead, well, at least Carly hadn't taken a piece of apple to the forehead.

I spent the next few hours surfing the Internet, looking at names. Jimmy Z. Landry, Zeke Stenner, Shayna Barnes, Billy Caldwell, Benny Barnes, Odell Barnabas. Resulted in a handful of nothing.

I was just getting off the computer when I heard the front door open.

Julianne was standing there, smiling at me. "Hello, househusband."

"What are you doing home?"

She tossed her briefcase on the sofa. "Funny. I expected to hear 'Wow. What a great surprise that you are home, instead of slaving away to support my big butt.'"

"That is what I meant to say."

"I figured." She shed her suit jacket. "I just assumed you might need some moral support before the big showdown tonight."

"I'm fine," I said. "I'm not easily frightened."

"I remember that one time you wouldn't kill the spider in the shower."

"That was a big freakin' spider."

"The size of a quarter, as I recall." She kicked off her pumps. "Nonetheless, I thought a little relaxation before the meeting might help."

"Okay."

She stood there, amusement in her eyes as she stared me down.

"What?" I asked.

"Were you this lame when we first started dating?"

"That feels like some sort of trick question."

She started undoing the buttons in the middle of her blouse as she backpedaled toward the stairs. "I came home early from work. To seduce my husband. Because I felt like it." She popped open the last button, pivoted, and started up the stairs. "Problem with that?"

"None whatsoever," I said, finally getting over my lameness and moving at double time toward the stairs.

46

"Seriously. Why did you take the afternoon off?" I asked.

We were still lying in bed, naked and twisted in the sheets like a couple of pretzels.

She brushed the brown locks of hair away from her eyes. "I needed a reason?"

"Usually you do. Don't get me wrong. This is way better than a phone call. But sometimes I can't even get you on the phone."

She wrapped her fingers into mine. "I had an appointment outside the office. I decided not to go back. And I wanted to make sure you weren't getting yourself into some sort of trouble."

Good thing she hadn't come home a couple hours earlier, then, when Victor and I were playing detective.

"Plus, I was afraid of what might happen to you if I sent you to the meeting by yourself again," she said, grinning.

"Thinking I might wear a helmet."

"Oh yeah. One of those Viking ones, with horns. Make a statement."

"That way I could impale Sharon Ann."

"I'm totally getting turned on by this."

We both laughed.

It was good to see her in the middle of the day, rid of the stress that went with her job. She was undertaking a huge sacrifice for our family by agreeing to be the breadwinner. Not just the working part, but missing out on spending the entire day with Carly. There were days where I felt guilty, but I wasn't entirely sure how to rectify it. We'd grown accustomed to a lifestyle that I didn't have the earning capacity to support. I knew that, realistically, we were doing the right thing for Carly and the three of us, but some days it felt more right than others.

That afternoon it felt about as right as it got.

"I saw Billy this morning," she said, stretching her long legs and pointing her toes like a cat.

I kissed her neck. "That is a mood killer."

"He wanted to know if we wanted to settle."

I stopped in midkiss. "I got the same offer."

"I offered him a dollar," she explained. "But then I rescinded."

"Nice work."

"He's gonna need a little more proof that you are a psycho to get any money out of me," she said.

"My mother told me something interesting."

"What's that?"

I told her about Shayna's alleged make-out fest with Billy.

"I don't really find that surprising," Julianne said.

"I didn't either," I said. "Makes me feel badly for Benny, though."

"The guy who permanently damaged you and then got blood all over our van?"

"Come on. When he hit me, it was clean. Part of playing football. And I don't think he had any say in wherever who killed him placed his body."

"He chose Shayna," Julianne said. "He knew what he was getting."

She was right, of course. But it didn't mean that a small part of me didn't feel some sympathy for the guy. I didn't know what had been going on in his life, but it seemed clear that none of it had been good.

"Both of them hate you, Deuce," she said. "And Benny probably did, too. I couldn't care less about any of them. I'm sorry someone killed Benny, but you didn't do it and you have nothing to be sorry about." She tapped me on the chest. "And their retarded little restraining order is just one more thing for the WORMS to throw at you."

I cut my eyes sideways toward her. "Think things will be thrown?"

Julianne pushed up toward my ear. "Count on it."

47

I wanted to spend the rest of the afternoon and evening right where we were, but Julianne convinced me that missing my own hearing would not be beneficial.

That's why she's considered to be the smart one in our family.

So we showered and dressed. My stomach began to do flip-flops as we left the house, and I was surprised. I didn't think I'd be nervous, and I certainly didn't want to be nervous. But I'd had a bad week, and I knew most of it was going to be put on display for all to see. I didn't like that, and as much as I wanted to play it cool, the anxiety was hammering away at me.

"Could you speed it up?" I asked Julianne.

We were in her little Lexus SC. It was the antithesis of the minivan. Sporty, fast, and cool. The car was the one completely selfish and irresponsible gift Julianne bought herself when she made partner. She'd grown up driving old pickups, and she'd promised herself that when she was able, she'd buy any car she wanted, and she settled on the Lexus.

The only uncool thing about the car was the way she drove it. About five miles under the posted speed limit at all times, keeping approximately 670 feet between her and the car in front of her, barking at anyone that dared to close within that distance from behind. She might as well have had the hazards on all the time. I wanted to replace the speedometer with a sundial, but I wasn't handy enough to know how to do it.

As usual, she ignored me. "Don't let them goad you into an argument up there, all right?"

A horse and buggy passed us. "I'm not going to get into an argument."

"Just stay with what we've talked about," she said, glancing in the rearview mirror. "I'll keep my mouth shut until it's time for me to get involved."

"How will I know when that is?"

"When I start talking."

"Right."

Two cars swerved around us and sped past, one saluting us with a middle finger.

"So rude," Julianne said.

"Well, if you actually pressed down on the accelerator . . ."

"You are rude, too."

"Rude is holding up traffic."

"Rude is not being polite to your wife after she's just spent the afternoon in bed with you and is coming to support you at a public flogging," she said.

Incredibly tough to argue with that.

After she'd turned a fifteen-minute drive into a

thirty-minute cruise, we finally pulled into the Rettler-Mott parking lot. As far away from all the other cars as was physically possible. Would probably take us another half an hour to reach the building.

She reached for my hand. "Don't be nervous. You are the best Room Dad ever."

"We should've worn shirts that said that."

"And I won't let anyone crack you over the head until we get inside tonight."

I thought I saw a glimpse of a smile on her face as she slid out of the car.

I was staring at the ground, thinking about what I wanted to say, when Julianne came to a halt and gripped my hand tight. "Who is *that?*"

I looked up. Parked in the row of cars closest to the school, leaning against an old station wagon, was Odell Barnabas.

"Oh. That's Odell," I said.

"You actually know him?" she asked, pressing in closer to me. "Seriously? My God. What is on his head?"

Odell saw us and pushed himself off the wagon. He yanked the toothpick out of his mouth and tossed it on the ground. He stuck his thumbs in the front pockets of his jeans and lifted his chin in our direction. "What's goin' on, y'all?"

"Hey, Odell," I said. "What are you doing here?"

"Lookin' for you, Ace. Heard you had a little deal here tonight," he said, his eyes making their way toward Julianne. "This your lady?"

"No, this is my wife," I said, glancing at Julianne. Her eyes were firmly ensconced on the toupee.

Odell chuckled and wrinkled his nose. "Sure, sure. Looks like a cool chick."

Julianne was too entranced by the fake hair to realize he was speaking about her like she was an inanimate object.

"So," Odell said, moving his eyes back to me. "You make up your mind yet?"

"Make up my mind?"

He rolled his eyes like I was the most forgetful human being he'd ever encountered. "On Killer Kids, Ace. Killer Kids."

"Ah, right," I said. "Think I'm gonna have to pass, Odell."

His hopeful expression crashed. "Come on. You don't wanna do that, Ace. It's gonna be huge."

"Gonna have to be huge without me, Odell. Just not my thing."

His lips twisted in disappointment. Then he raised his eyebrows. "Maybe you could be a silent partner. You know, just invest, but not do anything? Like I said, I've already got a couple of those. Then you'll still get rich when we all get rich."

His ignorance was almost sweet.

"Afraid not, Odell," I said, pulling on Julianne. She stumbled a bit, her eyes still examining his hair. "I think I'll just have to watch you and everyone else get rich."

He looked like a six-year-old who had all of his toys taken away.

"We've got to get inside," I said, motioning at the building. Julianne slowly moved her feet forward, but her eyes stayed put. "But I did want to ask you something."

Odell shrugged, as if he could care less now that I had removed myself from his plans.

"You told me the other day you had something going on with Shayna," I said. "Did you sleep with her?"

He bit down on his upper lip, and color flushed through his cheeks. "Hey, man, you know. A gentleman doesn't kiss and tell, okay, Ace? I told you the other day—"

"No, you didn't," I said, staring at him. "You didn't tell me anything. You wanted me to think you and Shayna had something going on, but you never explicitly said you did. So I wanna know. Did you?"

He chewed on the lip a bit more urgently and started cracking his knuckles. "Hey, Ace, if you—"

"Odell. I want an answer. Yes or no. Did you and Shayna sleep together?"

I thought I heard Julianne whisper, "It can't be real," but I wasn't sure.

Odell shuffled his feet and mumbled something I couldn't understand.

"What did you say, Odell?"

The feet shuffled again, and he let out a sigh. "No. We didn't sleep together. She turned me down."

Finally. Something made sense. I didn't care how crazy or drunk Shayna was, I knew she and Odell Barnabas had not slept together.

"But she *was* sleeping with that other fella at the store," he said with the tone of a defiant teenager.

"Yeah, Odell. That would've been her *husband.* Because she was *married* to him."

Julianne pulled me toward the building. "We're going to be late."

Odell frowned and shook his head. "No, Ace—"

"We gotta go," I said, cutting him off and continuing to move with Julianne toward the school. I didn't want to be late to this thing, and I'd had enough of Odell. "We'll see you around."

48

The auditorium at Rettler-Mott School was almost full by the time Julianne and I walked in. Our presence set off a buzz inside the room, as row after row of heads turned back in our direction.

"I'm going to have questions about that guy when this is over," Julianne whispered.

I wasn't sure I had the answers. Everyone who was anyone in Rose Petal was there. Sally Meadows was tucked back in a corner with several of her fellow teachers. Detective Willie Bell was leaning against the back wall. Darlene Andrews was in the second row, poured into some sort of velour outfit, her hair teased approximately six feet into the air. Mitch McCutcheon gave a short wave from his seat in the first row. Lots of other faces that I knew.

I didn't think that the room was choosing sides. This wasn't that kind of showdown. They were there simply to see what happened and to report back to the others who weren't fortunate enough to attend in person.

Sharon Ann McCutcheon was whispering into

Deborah Wilbon's ear from a row of folding chairs behind a podium. Several other of the WORMS filled the remaining chairs, Sharon Ann and Deborah sitting in the middle of them. Sharon Ann noticed us, said one last thing to Deborah, which caused her to turn her head in our direction, stood, and approached us.

"Hello, Deuce," she said through a forced smile, as if someone was pinching her rear end. "Hello, Julianne."

The dynamic between Sharon Ann and Julianne had always been strange. Julianne had attempted to be friends with her when Mitch first brought her back to Rose Petal, because Mitch and I were friends. But it became immediately clear that Sharon Ann had no intention of taking up that friendship, at least not in a sincere form. I was never sure exactly what Sharon Ann envied the most about my wife—her looks, her career, her family—but it was as obvious as a horse on roller skates. Sharon Ann was jealous of Julianne.

"Sharon Ann," said Julianne, looking past her at the other women sitting near the podium. "That's it?"

Sharon Ann ran a hand down her blouse, smoothing it out, though it was tough to smooth out that kind of plastic surgery. "That's it what?"

"I only count five of your little friends," Julianne said. "You're going to need more than that."

Sharon Ann bristled. "I think we'll be fine."

Julianne stared at her for a long moment, then gave a little shrug. "All right. Your choice." She looked at me. "This is going to be easier than I expected."

Sharon Ann's lips fastened together in an irritated grimace. I couldn't tell whether Julianne was being serious or if she was just trying to stick it to Sharon Ann and get inside her head. If I knew my wife even the tiniest bit, it was probably a little of both.

Sharon Ann's eyes narrowed, in much the same way I assumed a shark's did before it attacked its prey. "I'd like to get started. Are you ready?"

I looked at Julianne, who was returning the narrow-eyed shark stare at Sharon Ann. Her head tilted forward in a tight, confident nod.

I was glad someone was confident.

"Okay then," I said, taking another long look around the room, wondering who, if anyone, was rooting for me. "I guess we're ready."

49

When I was a kid, my parents served as copresidents of the parent-teacher association at my elementary school. At their final meeting at the end of their two-year term, my father put a man named Charles Spillner in a headlock because he'd had the poor idea to say that he thought my parents had done a lousy job. As my father brought him to the front of the room in the headlock, my mother presided over the swearing in of the new officers.

The Spillners' daughter, Andrea, never spoke to me again.

So when I thought of any type of parent-teacher school meeting, I couldn't get the image of my father locking up Charlie Spillner out of my head. As I watched Sharon Ann up at the podium, I hoped that headlocks would not be necessary on this night.

Sharon Ann cleared her throat and tapped the microphone attached to the wooden podium. Her face morphed into a sea of warmth and friendliness, all the Botox in her face coagulating its way into a gigantic smile.

"Good evening, friends," she said, letting her eyes sweep the room, as if each and every person there was her personal friend. "We all appreciate your attendance here this evening in regard to this important matter." She shuffled through several sheets of paper in front of her. "As most of you know, Mr. Deuce Winters serves as the Room Mother. . . ."

She pursed her lips together and again let her eyes sweep the room, feigning embarrassment. "Excuse me. I meant to say Room Father."

She, in fact, meant to say exactly what she said. It was her subtle way of letting the room know that I was miscast in the role from the get-go.

"And he has served admirably in that role for the majority of the school year," Sharon Ann continued. "We all certainly appreciate his efforts on behalf of the children in room nine."

A slight murmur arose from the room, and I couldn't tell if it was positive or negative.

"But at this time I feel it is my unfortunate duty to request that Mr. Winters be replaced in his current position," Sharon Ann said, adopting a seriousness normally reserved for funerals and beauty pageants.

She cut her eyes in my direction. "Unless, of course, Mr. Winters would prefer to save us all the trouble and resign his current position."

I had to hand it to Sharon Ann. She knew how to work a room.

I stood and faced the room. "I have no intention of resigning my position." I turned, smiled at Sharon Ann, and sat down.

A brief flash of anger rocketed through Sharon Ann's eyes as the crowd murmured again. She quickly composed herself, though, and put on an expression of resigned disappointment, as if that was what she'd expected. "Then I guess we should get the proceedings under way since Mr. Winters does not wish to step aside."

Maybe I *would* need to put Sharon Ann in a headlock.

She glanced at Deborah and the other three women now sitting behind her. They all nodded assuredly at one another, portraying the confidence of people who were about to present a can't-miss cure for cancer.

Sharon Ann shuffled through the papers once again. "At this time I would like to formally recommend Mr. Winters's removal as Room Father for room nine. Do I hear a second?"

Deborah and the others behind her all chimed in with "Seconded." It was clear that they had rehearsed.

Sharon Ann suppressed a smile. "Excellent. At this time we do not feel that Mr. Winters—"

"Who's we, Sharon Ann?" Julianne asked.

The room murmured again.

"The Women of Rettler-Mott School, Julianne," Sharon Ann said through clenched teeth.

"So it's the group that's recommending this action?" Julianne asked, the amused smile from before again creeping across her face.

Sharon Ann met her question with irritation. "That is correct."

Julianne nodded, satisfied. "Excellent. Continue."

Sharon Ann started to spit something, most likely because she didn't like Julianne giving her permission to run her own meeting. But she bit her tongue, attempting to stay focused. "As I was saying, we are making this recommendation due to the recent troubles that Mr. Winters has experienced."

The murmuring in the room got louder, and Sharon Ann was happy to let it fester.

"He is an active suspect in an ongoing murder investigation," Sharon Ann said, pausing to let that settle in with the audience. "And he has recently been served with a restraining order after harassing the wife of the victim." She shifted her gaze to the middle of the auditorium, and I followed it.

Shayna and Billy were sitting together. Shayna's head was down. Billy was patting her on the back.

Rose Petal seriously needed to give thought to the idea of forming a community theater, because there was some amazing acting talent in the town.

Sharon Ann did a little head shake, clearly displeased with me. "Clearly, Mr. Winters has other issues in his life right now that would seem to prevent him from performing his duties."

My blood pressure did zero to sixty in less than two seconds. Even though I had prepared myself for what she was going to say, hearing it out loud, in front of all those people, was like another shot to the head.

Julianne's hand pressed down on mine.

"We wanna see Deuce!" Darlene yelled from behind us.

I cringed as the entire room went silent.

"I mean, we wanna hear from Deuce," Darlene

corrected herself, but not blushing. "We wanna hear what he has to say."

Sharon Ann's mouth twitched. "Certainly." She looked at me. "You may express any wishes you have against this going forward." She turned back toward the audience. "Though I doubt it will matter."

I stood and walked to the lecturn. It would've been the ideal moment for a headlock, but I decided against it.

I spotted Cedric near the back of the room, working a toothpick between his lips. "Sheriff. Am I a suspect?"

"Not in my book," Cedric said, grinning.

Judge Gerald Kantner was right next to him, yawning.

"Judge, did the restraining order present any evidence that I harassed anyone?" I asked.

Gerald shook his head. "No, Deuce, it did not. That is why the order was granted with temporary status. If cause had been presented, then I would have considered a more stringent order."

And then I had to take a chance. "Detective Bell."

He was startled to hear his name called, and he straightened against the wall.

"Anyone file a complaint with you, complaining about me?" I asked.

The entire room turned in his direction.

The pink splotches that I'd seen before were forming on his face. He didn't like being the center of attention.

"No," he said quietly.

"Can you say that again?" I asked. "So everyone can hear you?"

"No," he said, louder and more irritated.

The murmurs grew into voices, clearly surprised. I turned around to Sharon Ann. Her cheeks were drawn tight; her jaw set firm. She wasn't enjoying her meeting.

I turned back to the room. "Sally. You still want me as your Room Dad?"

Sally Meadows stood and was already nodding. "Absolutely. I have no complaints."

The murmuring came to life again.

"Thanks," I said.

Sally saluted and sat down.

"My daughter loves this school," I said to the crowd. "I love being able to help out with her class. I believe her teacher, Ms. Meadows, is happy with the job I've done as Room Dad." I took a long look across the room, trying to catch as many eyes as possible. "I do not have any plans to leave the job before my term is up. Thank you."

Applause started in the back of the room and worked its way forward. I was feeling pretty good about the moment. I took my seat back next to Julianne. She patted my hand, proud. Never underestimate the power of a high school football hero in Texas.

Sharon Ann and Deborah were in a tight-lipped, white-faced discussion as the applause continued. Sharon Ann finally stood and returned to the podium.

"Well, it is lovely to hear that Mr. Winters has been able to clear his name. To a certain extent, of course," she said with all the friendliness of a python. "Of course, there is another issue I'd like to bring up before we vote."

The room came to attention.

"Two nights ago," Sharon Ann said, "Mr. Winters was attacked out in front of the school. Fortunately, he is all right. The attack, however, raises a concern."

My confidence was disappearing by the second. I didn't like her standing up there, looking like she was about to swing a big hammer right at my head.

"Whether or not he is to blame for the attack, it does concern me that someone is out to get him," she said, pausing like a well-rehearsed orator. "Particularly when he is around the children."

That set off the murmurs again and blew my confidence into itty-bitty pieces. Sharon Ann was very pleased with herself, trying to hold off a smug smile. She looked down at her papers as it started to broaden across her face, like a kid who didn't want to get caught laughing in the back of the class.

She managed to wipe the smile from her face for a moment and held up her hands for quiet. "I think you understand where I'm coming from. We do not want to put our children at risk." She glanced around the room. "And I would be happy to sacrifice my time in order to take his place. So that our children can remain safe."

"Good God," Julianne whispered. "Like she's willing to hold off the plague or something."

"I'm done," I whispered above the conversations behind us. "She got me."

Julianne raised an eyebrow. "Not even close, househusband. Not even close."

"Jules, she's got everyone drinking the Kool-Aid," I said, gesturing behind us.

Julianne frowned and looked back to Sharon Ann.

"So I think it's time we vote," Sharon Ann said,

her chin upraised, her fake boobs puffed out in victory. "Should Mr. Winters be replaced as Room Father of room nine?"

Julianne stood. "Don't waste their time, Sharon Ann."

Sharon Ann's eyes turned into tiny little AK-47s, firing in my wife's direction. "I'm not wasting their time, Julianne. Now I'm sorry your husband . . ."

"You are sorry," Julianne said. "I think we may need to recall you as president of the WOR . . . Women of Rettler-Mott."

Sharon Ann reloaded the AK-47s. "Oh, really. And why would that be?"

"Because you don't even know your own bylaws, honey," Julianne said, now facing the audience.

Sharon Ann blinked her eyes several times. Any other moment, it would've looked like she was batting her eyelashes at someone. But I saw it as doubt sneaking its way into her pea brain.

"How many women are in the group?" Julianne asked, still watching the audience, in full lawyer mode now. "In the Women of Rettler-Mott?"

Sharon Ann started to say something, then caught herself. She turned to Deborah and the three women behind her, covering the microphone. Her colleagues met her with shrugs.

When she turned back around, her cheeks were pink and she wasn't pleased about having to stare at the back of Julianne's head. "I'm not sure, but I don't see any way that's relevant."

Julianne smiled at the audience, full of confidence. "Again. I'd think someone in your position would know your own bylaws."

The decibel level of the murmurs rose, the crowd sensing something big was about to go down.

"Let's take a guess, then," Julianne said, turning around to face Sharon Ann. "Two, twenty, two hundred? As president of the Women of Rettler-Mott, how many women do you think you preside over?"

The pink in Sharon Ann's cheeks blossomed. "If I had to guess, I'd say forty. Certainly not more than fifty, and two hundred is ludicrous." It was a poor attempt to save face.

"Forty," Julianne said, nodding as if that was fine. "Let's go with that."

Sharon Ann twitched with irritation. "Honestly, Julianne. You are wasting everyone's time. This is ridiculous."

Julianne upped the wattage in her smile. "It's on page four of the school bylaws."

"What is?"

"The part that says in order for any parent-sponsored group to make a change of any kind that the group must present at least fifty-one percent of their group for a public vote," Julianne said, turning back to the audience.

The murmurs rose to a few chuckles and whistles. I made out a few "Uh-ohs" and "That woman is screweds."

Sharon Ann's face rippled from pink to strawberry red. "That is nonsense! I would know something like that if it were true."

Julianne whipped out a small royal blue book and held it up. "Well, I certainly would've thought you would've known something like that before putting on this dog and donkey show." She tossed the book at her. "Page four, Sharon Ann. It's the one that comes after page three. We'll go ahead and wait for you to read it."

Sharon Ann attempted to catch the booklet but missed it completely, and it whacked her in the chin. Twenty-three percent of the audience laughed. She bent over, picked it up, and ripped through the pages. When her face went from strawberry red to a four-alarm fire, it was clear that she had somehow skipped over page four of the Rettler-Mott bylaws.

Julianne put a hand to her ear. "Can't hear you, Sharon Ann. Did you find it yet?"

Sharon Ann was scouring the booklet, searching vainly for an out. It wasn't there.

"And before you get any ideas about trying to get fifty-one percent of the women together," Julianne cautioned, "I've already made a few phone calls. I'm not sure what the vote here tonight would be like, but the chances of you getting fifty-one percent here are slim and none, and none just kicked slim out of town." She smiled her most evil smile. "Seems my husband has a few more friends in this school than you do."

The whistles from the audience morphed into catcalls, along with some sporadic applause. Sharon Ann stood at the podium like a dog that had just had its teeth removed. Without anesthesia. People were standing up to leave, and there was nothing she could do but watch.

Julianne held out her hand. "Let's go, my man."

I grabbed her hand and stood.

Sharon Ann fumbled around behind the podium

for a moment, grabbing her purse and whispering violently in Deborah's ear.

Sharon Ann McCutcheon made the one mistake of not knowing the one thing I was most certain of in my life.

My wife kicks so much ass.

50

Most men probably would've had an issue with their wife defending them in public.

Please. That is so sexist.

"I have a serious mind to jump your bones right here in this parking lot," I told her as we walked out.

"Now, that might actually be cause to remove you," she said, grinning at me. "Let's wait until we get home."

"Can we at least make out in your car?"

"Deal."

And that's what we did for a good five minutes before coming up for air.

"How was that?" Julianne whispered in the same throaty tone she'd used the first time she asked me stay over in her dorm room.

I was about to answer her with another round of kissing, but a car leaving the parking lot caught my eye.

Specifically, a red Ford Ranger pickup truck leaving caught my eye.

Julianne punched me in the sternum. "Hey. I'm trying to be all attractive to you, you idiot."

"Uh-huh," I said, watching the truck creep along the opposite side of the parking lot.

Julianne saw my eyes were elsewhere and turned in her seat. "What?"

"That truck," I said, squinting. "It's the truck Victor saw."

"The one he got the partial plate on?"

"Yeah. He found that Stenner kid who owns it, but we don't think he was the one driving it," I said as its red brake lights flared in the dark as it arrived at the edge of the lot.

She twisted back around to me. "How do you know all this?"

"Victor and I," I said, watching the truck turn out onto the street. "We, uh . . ." I pointed to the truck. "Come on. We need to go after it."

"You're kidding me."

I smacked the dash. "Come on, Jules. Now."

She made a grunting sound but turned over the ignition and backed out of the parking spot, following in the direction the truck had gone.

"You and Victor are buddies now?" she asked, hitting the accelerator.

I watched the road in front of us, the taillights on the pickup coming into view. "We're not buddies."

"Then what exactly are you?"

"We're sort of . . . partners."

She cut her eyes to me. "You're what?"

"Watch the road," I said.

"You better start explaining yourself, Deuce Winters," she said, focusing back on the road.

"I helped him do a little investigating," I said. I gestured at the windshield. "Come on. Faster."

"I am driving fast."

For her, that was true. But I expected a toddler on a Big Wheel to fly by us at any moment.

The pickup came to a halt at a red light and allowed us to catch up. I could make out two people in the car, but all I saw was the backs of two heads and those were obscured by the headrests, to the point that I couldn't even tell the gender of either person.

"Start talking, Deuce, or I swear I will stop this car dead in the street," Julianne said, her needle hitting her own personal redline. "And then kick you out into it."

I reluctantly told her about all Victor and I had done during the day. As the light turned green, my wife's face was turning bright red.

"You are such an idiot," she said, easing the Lexus forward, behind the pickup.

"I know that."

"No, you don't. Because if you realized what an idiot you're behaving like, you'd hit yourself in the head."

I doubted I would ever hit myself in the head.

I was trying to think of an appropriate response when the pickup shot forward, nearly doubling the speed it had been traveling at before.

"Go!" I said, leaning forward in my seat.

Julianne increased our speed by approximately three miles an hour, and the taillights were getting smaller in front of us.

"Jules, please!"

She muttered something under her breath, but the Lexus engine roared and we jerked forward.

The pickup hung a hard right, the rear bed fish-tailing wildly behind it. Four seconds later Julianne turned the Lexus around the corner as if she was driving her normal speed.

I doubted that my minivan would've cornered so well.

"Are we really in a car chase?" Julianne asked, her tone somewhere between disbelief and excitement.

"They obviously spotted your car behind them," I said.

"Obviously."

We were on a street that was bordered on the left by a neighborhood of homes and on our right by horse pasture. Julianne pressed the accelerator again, and our headlights came up on the rear end of the truck. I didn't want to stop the truck. I just wanted to see who was inside.

And whoever was in there very clearly wanted to make sure that we saw nothing.

The truck swung right and jumped the curb. It crashed through a three-line barbed-wire fence and into the pasture. A group of horses scattered in all directions as the truck came toward them.

Julianne hit the brakes, and the Lexus rocked to a stop. "Not a chance I'm following them through there."

I didn't expect her to follow the truck into the pasture, but I was disappointed as the truck crossed the pasture and disappeared over a berm. I knew the other side of the pasture was bordered by another street, and by the time we got over there, the truck would be long gone.

"I'm sorry," Julianne said, touching my arm. "I'm really disappointed."

I threw my head back against the seat. "I know. Me, too. I just feel like there's something with that truck. Knowing Victor saw it in the lot the other night and now seeing it again . . ."

"No, that's not what I meant," Julianne said.

"What did you mean?"

"I'm really disappointed that not once did you yell, 'Follow that car!'"

51

I woke up the next morning not feeling nearly as good as I figured I would.

After taking down Sharon Ann and her cronies and retaining my Room Dad responsibilities, I thought I'd be flying high. But now, after the day Victor and I had and after another visit from the red pickup, I was more on edge. I wasn't celebrating my victory. I was waiting for the next battle.

Which, you know, was really dumb, because I was a stay-at-home dad in a town called Rose Petal, and it wasn't like I was some sort of superhero out looking for trouble.

But whatever.

Julianne, as usual, was out the door early, probably attempting to make up for being out of the office the afternoon before. After I showered, dressed, and ate, I drove to my parents to pick up Carly.

She was sitting between my parents on their front porch swing, her hair in pigtails, her backpack strapped over her shoulders, and her Dora lunch box perched in her lap. Julianne and I enjoyed the freedom we had in being able to drop her at my parents for afternoons or overnights, but every time I saw her after she'd been gone for a night, I realized how much I missed having her chasing around my heels in the house.

She jumped off the swing and hopped down the stairs, my mother warning her not to get dirty. I swung her up and kissed her cheek. "Hello, dude."

"I'm not a dude," she said, pulling back and looking at me like I was crazy.

"That's right. You're a dinosaur."

"I'm a girl, Daddy."

I kissed her again. "If you say so."

My mother stood and came down the stairs. My father remained in his lounging position on the swing.

"She behave herself?" I asked.

"Of course," my mother said. "She was perfect."

I knew she wasn't, but she could've set fire to the house and then stabbed a random farm animal and my mother would've told me she behaved herself.

"Beat down all those women last night, huh?" my father called from the porch.

I raised a hand. "Victory."

"Never thought you had it in you."

"Then you thought wrong."

"I meant I didn't think you had being a Room Daddy in you," he said with a sly grin.

An attempt to flip him the bird was squashed as my mother smacked my wrist before I could get the finger extended, so we said our good-byes and headed off to school.

Sally Meadows met me at the door to her classroom with a big smile. "Nice to see you this morning."

"I would've been here, regardless."

She bent down and gave Carly a hug. "Good morning, Miss Carly."

Carly, as usual, said a quick good morning and scampered into the room to begin her day.

Sally stood. "And as much as I'd like to let you enjoy your victory, I think I'm going to have to ruin it."

"Why's that?"

She glanced at her classroom before looking back to me. "I need you to run an errand for me. In your Room Dad capacity."

"Of course. That's what I'm here for."

"The T-shirts are done," she explained. "For Play Day."

Play Day was the next to last day of the school year, where the kids participated in a kind of preschool Olympics. Each classroom competed as their own country, and though I had yet to witness it, it sounded hilarious and I looked forward to seeing Carly and her classmates compete as Team Turkey.

"Okay, cool," I said.

"So I'd like for you to pick them up if you could," she said. "I need to make sure they fit, make sure they look all right and all that."

"Sure. I can go get them. Where are they at?"

The smile on her face wilted. "Sharon Ann's."

Why not just kick me in the shins?

"You're kidding me," I said.

She shook her head. "She had a printing connection, remember? So she got the shirts done. And Mitch was the one who came to school this morning, and he didn't bring them."

That made sense. Sharon Ann probably had no

intention of showing her face after going down in public flames.

"But I really would like to have those shirts, Deuce," Sally said, wincing as if asking me was painful for her.

"No problem," I said. "I'll go get them."

She raised her eyebrows. "Really? You don't mind?"

"It's my job. It'll be fine. We're all adults," I told her, not for a moment believing that Sharon Ann would act like an adult.

52

Rose Petal actually sits on a strip of diagonal land between two large lakes. Lake Taitano to the south and Lake Gentry to the north. The McCutcheons lived out on the southern shore of Lake Gentry, one of the most prime pieces of real estate in not just Rose Petal, but in all of North Texas. The homes were behind gates, walking trails wound beneath huge Spanish oaks, and people drove by, wishing they were going home rather than just wondering what was behind those gates.

The gentleman at the guardhouse made a quick call after I told him who I was there to see. After hanging up the phone, he gave me a polite wave and the massive iron gates swung open, an invitation to enter.

I'd been to Mitch and Sharon Ann's several times. They played host to numerous charity events in Rose Petal, and Julianne and I had been invited to them. Before I'd impeded on her territory at the preschool, she publicly pretended to like us and therefore included us on her party invitation list. That had, of course, all changed, and after the previous evening, I was certain it had changed again for the worst.

Their home was a sprawling two-story mini-mansion, complete with faux pillars in front of the entryway and a semicircular cobblestone drive. The perfectly mown lawn ran down to the edge of the lake that kissed the back of their home. Selling cars was a good way to make a lot of money, apparently.

I parked the minivan in the drive and walked up to the huge oak double doors, sticking my finger on the doorbell. Chimes echoed behind the doors, and a shadow grew larger behind the smoked glass slats in the middle of the doors.

The door on the right opened, and Sharon Ann was standing there wearing khaki capris, a sleeveless white blouse, and a painful, fake smile. “Hello, Deuce.”

“Hello, Sharon Ann.”

“Won’t you come in?”

It was a testament to her Southern upbringing that she was inviting me inside her home. Even as angry as I assumed she was with me, her manners and hospitality did not take a backseat.

I walked into the entryway of marble floors and raised ceilings. The pleasant aroma of citrus wafted through the air. Not a single square inch of the home was anything but gleaming.

Sharon Ann worked her cleaning ladies hard.

“Sally called and said you’d be stopping by for the shirts,” she said, shutting the door behind me. “I’ve got them out here in the kitchen.”

I followed her into the expansive kitchen that looked out over both a huge oval pool and the lake.

Maybe Mitch was able to tolerate her because the views were so magnificent.

She pointed at two square cardboard cartons on the island in the middle of the kitchen. "There they are."

I pulled back the flap on one of the boxes. Light blue T-shirts, a silhouette of the country of Turkey in the middle, with a small turkey in the middle of the silhouette. "These look great."

Sharon Ann nodded, her lips pressed tightly together, her eyes bouncing from the box to me to the box and back to me. She tapped her long red nails against the slate on top of the island.

"I'm not going to apologize," she said finally.

"I didn't expect you to."

"I was doing what I thought was right. What I still think is right."

I folded the flap back on the box, closing it up. "Sharon Ann, if I ever thought for a second that anything I was doing in any way put any child in danger, I'd stay at least a hundred miles away from the school. But I like participating in my daughter's class, and not you or anyone else is going to prevent me from doing that. You don't have to like it, but you better understand it."

We were locked in a stare down when her phone rang. She grabbed the cordless and answered it.

"Hello? Oh, hi, Deb." She smiled at me, as if Deborah calling her proved something. "What? You're what? What are you talking about?" She blinked several times, then covered the mouthpiece. "Excuse me, Deuce." She walked out of the kitchen and down the hallway, her voice lowered as she spoke into the phone.

I had to hand it to her. She had the polite thing on autopilot.

I checked the contents of each box, matching up the numbers of shirts and their sizes with the packing list in each box. If the shirts were any indicator, Turkey would be a heavy favorite in the preschool Olympics.

Sharon Ann returned to the kitchen, the phone in her hand and an irritated expression on her face. She set the phone on the island, next to the boxes. "I'm sorry about that."

"Everything okay?" I asked.

She started to say something, caught herself, and straightened her posture. "Thank you for coming by, Deuce."

A polite way of telling me to get lost.

"Not a problem," I said, grabbing the boxes and sliding them off the island.

The corner of the second box, though, caught the phone and knocked it to the floor, sending it clattering across the brushed concrete.

Sharon Ann folded her arms across her chest and pursed her lips.

"Sorry about that," I said, setting the boxes down, angry with myself for feeling like an idiot.

I bent down and picked the phone up from under the cabinet. I took a quick look at it to make sure I hadn't busted it.

The last number from the last call, the one Sharon had walked out of the room to take, was on the readout, the name registered to the number across the top of the digits. I stared at it for a long moment, then rose and handed the phone over to Sharon Ann.

"I'll let you know if it's broken," she said, barely

looking at the phone as she set it back in the cradle. She stared at me for a moment, taking a deep breath, not bothering to hide the fact that she wasn't happy I was still there. "Did you want something else, Deuce?"

My eyes were glued to the phone. She followed my gaze. "Are you worried about the phone? I'm sure it's fine. We drop it all the time."

I didn't say anything.

Sharon Ann rolled her eyes, stomped to the island, picked up the boxes, and held them out to me. I took them, started to say something, then stopped.

She put her hand on the small of my back and guided me back toward the entryway, opening the massive front door.

I stepped through the door and turned around, clutching the boxes. "That was Deborah on the phone?"

"Not that it's any of your business," she said, placing a hand on her hip, "but, yes, it was Deborah. Good-bye, Deuce." She shut the door a little harder than necessary, the slam echoing across the cul-de-sac.

I walked slowly toward the minivan, the boxes balanced carefully in my arms, my mind spinning.

I hadn't meant to knock the phone to the floor, but that small accident now had me more confused than ever.

Sharon Ann said it was Deborah on the line, and I had no reason to doubt her. I'd heard the beginning of the conversation. She probably called Sharon Ann half a dozen times a day. Her calling was nothing out of the ordinary.

But where she was calling from . . . well, that was the confusing part.

I opened the minivan and set the boxes of T-shirts on the floor, then closed the door and turned around to take another look at the McCutcheon home.

The readout indicated that Deborah was calling from Land O' Rugs.

53

I'd left my cell phone in the drink holder of the minivan, and it was beeping when I jumped into the driver's seat. I punched in the message code and listened to Victor telling me to call him back right away.

I did as directed.

"Doolittle," he answered.

"That's how you answer your phone?" I asked, starting the van and heading away from the McCutcheon home. "Doolittle? It's kind of rude."

"It's my last name, and it's not rude," he said, irritated. "Get over it. Where are you?"

"Picking up T-shirts. You?"

"Doing work you're gonna be happy to pay me for," he said. "When can you meet me?"

I had three hours until I needed to be back at the school. "Now's good."

"You know Louise's over in Lewisville?"

"Uh, yeah."

"See you there."

I set the phone back in the drink holder as I passed

the gatehouse and wondered why I was going to meet Victor Anthony Doolittle at Louise's.

Twenty minutes later I was pulling into the parking lot at Louise's Maternity Closet, DFW's largest maternity wear provider. Mannequins in the window were dressed in brightly colored dresses, showcasing their baby bellies in various states of pregnancy. Another mannequin sat in a chair, hooked up to a neon orange breast pump. Julianne and I had, in fact, purchased her breast pump at Louise's.

Pale yellow, not neon orange.

I pushed open the door to the store and saw Victor sitting in a chair near the counter, paging through a copy of *Pregnancy for Dummies.*

He looked up. "Hey."

A woman behind the counter smiled at me.

"Hey," I said. I pointed to the book. "Gonna invite me to the shower?"

He closed the book and set it on his lap. He pointed up at the woman behind the counter. "This is my sister. Louise."

Aha.

"Pleasure to meet you," she said.

"Same here."

Victor saw the expression on my face. "Just in case you're wondering, she's not a small person."

My cheeks warmed. "Thanks."

He pointed a stubby finger at one of the changing rooms. "And my girlfriend is in there. She's in her second trimester."

Victor Anthony Doolittle was spawning? That wouldn't be good for anyone.

He pushed himself off the floor. "Louise, you mind if he and I talk in the back?"

She busied herself with a thick ledger on the counter. "Don't steal anything."

He gestured for me to follow him, then stopped in front of the door of the dressing room that housed his girlfriend. "Jillian, I'll be back in a minute."

Whoever was behind the door murmured an assent.

I followed him through a narrow hallway and into a room that was no more than twelve by twelve. Boxes and wardrobe racks on wheels filled most of the space.

Victor motioned for me to close the door behind me, which I did.

"I don't like to do business in front of my girl," he said, shrugging. "Gets her all jumpy."

"Sure. Have, uh, you guys been together long?"

"Little over a year," he said.

"Know what the baby is?"

"Boy." He grinned. "Victor Junior."

God help us all.

"Did a little more digging on Zeke Stenner," Victor said, getting down to business. "The kid that owns the truck."

"I saw the truck again last night."

"Oh yeah?"

I recounted our chase from the parking lot to the horse pasture.

He processed all that, rubbing his chin. "It wasn't Stenner."

"How do you know?"

"Because I was watching him drinking with a couple of buddies at a bar near the university," he explained. "At that exact time."

That didn't really surprise me. I was certain after

pulling up on Stenner in the Tough Tykes parking lot that he wasn't after me for any reason.

"But I think his roommate might be the one using the truck," Victor said.

"His roommate?"

He nodded. "They live in an apartment complex about a mile from the school. I asked around a bit. Neighbors say his roommate borrows the truck all the time." His features screwed up, and he shook his head. "Which is so odd, because his roommate is loaded. Or at least the guy's father is. Local businessman who owns a couple of stores. Can't imagine why the kid would need to borrow anything, much less a truck."

"You find out his name?"

There was a knock on the door behind me.

Victor nodded, and his gaze moved past me. "Hey, baby."

I turned around. I wasn't sure what I was expecting.

Okay, that's not even close to being true. I was expecting a pregnant midget.

What I got was a supermodel.

Six feet at least, long golden hair, and longer legs. Perfect porcelain skin with aquamarine eyes. A small belly bump beneath the middle of a flowery sundress. Like she'd just walked off a magazine cover into Louise's back room.

"Victor, I'm ready," she said, smiling at him first, then me.

He wiggled a finger between us. "Jillian, Deuce. Deuce, Jillian."

We exchanged waves.

"Be done in one sec, baby," he said.

She gave a curt nod, then backed gracefully out of the room.

So completely *not* a pregnant midget.

Victor must've noticed whatever bewildered expression had settled on my face. "What?"

"Nothing. She's, uh . . . uh . . ."

"A goddamn knockout," he said. "You're not the only one who did well in the woman department."

I didn't know there was such a thing as the woman department, but I knew there was a compliment in there somewhere.

"And if you've got the bright idea to mention to Jillian about me flirting with your wife, forget about it," he said, waving his hand in the air. "She knows I'm an incorrigible flirt, all right? She also knows I'd never step out on her." He winked at me. "No matter how much your wife begged."

"Begged," I said. "Yeah, I'm sure that's how it'd go down."

He made a face. "You'd be surprised. Women find my height to be an aphrodisiac."

Which I found gave me a gag reflex.

"Anyway, yeah, I got the roommate's name," Victor said, moving on. "And where he works."

As he fished a scrap of paper out of his pocket, I pondered the ways he and Jillian might've met.

Match.com, maybe.

A personal ad.

Mutual friends.

Or perhaps she'd lost the biggest bet known to mankind.

"Here it is," Victor said, shaking out the piece of paper.

I shook myself out of my reverie in order to pay attention.

"You'll love this," Victor said, chuckling. "Kid manages one of his father's stores. A rug store in Lewisville."

All sorts of sparks fired inside my head.

"Stenner's roomate's name is Reggie Hamlin," Victor said, turning the sparks in my head into a genuine fire.

54

"Reggie?" I said.

"Yeah, why?" Victor said. "You know him?"

Victor told me before that coincidences were for people who tried to give pancakes to rats. That made no sense, but it was the only thing that I could think of.

"You look like you've seen a ghost," Victor said.

"Sort of feels that way."

"Care to explain?"

I told him about meeting Reggie at the rug store, about Benny working there, and about our conversation.

Victor rubbed his chin when I finished. "So why would this guy be after you?"

"No clue."

Which was true. Our conversation had been cordial, uneventful, and I'd walked away thinking nothing more about him other than he was mature for his age after he'd explained how he'd handled Benny and Odell. But coupled with the fact that Deborah Wilbon had just recently placed a call from Land O' Rugs, something was definitely not right at the friendly little community rug dealer.

Victor glanced at his watch. "I need to get rolling. Jillian and I have a doctor's appointment." He smiled. "Check on Victor Junior."

"Right."

"I'll make some calls," he said, walking back toward the front of the store. "You around tonight?"

"Should be, yeah."

"I'll call you later on, then."

I followed him back through the door and into the store.

Jillian was chatting with Louise. She smiled when she saw Victor. "You ready, honey?"

He walked over and kissed her hand, much in the same way he'd done to Julianne's when they'd met.

"Ready to take you home and make another baby," he growled.

Jillian dissolved into laughter. Louise rolled her eyes. I felt my breakfast trying to fight its way up my throat.

"Maybe later," she purred, placing a hand on his cheek. "We don't want to be late to the doctor."

I exchanged good-byes with Louise and followed the happy couple outside into the already warm morning air.

Victor scooted around the MG to open the door for Jillian. She gave me a quick wave before she slid gracefully into the sports car. Victor shut the door behind her and walked back to me.

"Don't go trying to be a hero," he said, pointing a finger at me.

"I won't," I said. "Wait. What do you mean?"

"Let me make some calls and see if I can get a

better handle on what's going on here," he said. "Don't go stepping in it before you know what you're stepping in."

"You gonna protect me?" I asked.

He stood his ground on the sidewalk, his expression serious, devoid of any of the smarmy cockiness I'd seen over the past few days.

"Quit being a wiseass," he said. "It's not about protecting you. It's about being smart." He adjusted the fedora. "I'll call you later." He stepped into the car, and he and his ridiculously attractive girlfriend zipped out of the lot.

Victor was, of course, correct. There was no sense in going to confront Reggie Hamlin at that very moment. Victor had proven himself very capable of rooting out information, which was starting to link a few things, if not tie them together with a cute little knot.

But there's something about knowing that some little punk running a rug store might've taken a potshot at the back of your head that blocks the pathway in the brain through which the "Don't do this!" message is sent to the rest of the body.

Really. It's a scientific fact.

55

I parked outside Land O' Rugs and gathered myself.

I had a lot of questions. I didn't want to go in there and get in a fight with Reggie, but I wanted some answers. I was thinking that maybe just by showing up, I'd catch him by surprise and he'd spill the entire story and then we'd all live happily ever after.

The first moment I knew that wasn't going to happen was when I opened the door to the store and saw Shayna Barnes grabbing her sister, Deborah Wilbon, by the hair. Deborah, clearly on the defensive, was trying to stick her nails in Shayna's eyes. Both were emitting high-pitched, indecipherable sounds as they rolled around on a pile of rugs just to the left of the entrance.

The appropriate thing to do would've been to wade into the fracas and separate them and calm everyone down and let them reclaim their senses.

Instead, I sat down on a pile of rugs and watched.

"I've hated you for twenty years!" Shayna yelled,

snapping Deborah's head back as she yanked harder on her hair.

"I've hated you my *whole life!*" Deborah screamed back, now both hands clawing at Shayna's face.

They rolled to the left, then back to the right.

"I can't believe you did it!" Shayna screeched. "You slut!"

"I learned it from you!" Deborah fired back.

Again to the left and back to the right. Shayna had Deborah's head pulled so far back, her neck was arched. Deborah's nails were so firmly implanted in Shayna's cheeks that it looked like she was stuck on her face.

As amusing as it all was, it wasn't doing anything for me.

"Ladies," I said.

Both of their heads snapped in my direction, different degrees of agony on each of their faces.

I held out my hand. "Don't get up. I didn't mean to intrude."

Neither let go of the other, but they glanced at each other, unsure of what to do now.

"You can't be near me," Shayna finally said. "The restraining order."

"Didn't know you were going to be here, Shayna."

"What are you doing here?" Shayna asked, trying to lock her arm stiff, with her hand on her sister's jaw.

"I'm looking for Reggie," I said.

"Aren't we all?" Deborah said, chopping Shayna's arm at the elbow. Shayna's arm gave, and Deborah scooted just out of her reach.

"Shut up, Deborah," Shayna spat, cutting her eyes to her sister.

"You shut up, Shayna."

Great. It was just like being at preschool.

They sat there, glaring at each other, breathing heavily. They each had long pink streaks on their arms and cheeks from where they'd dug into one another.

"So where is Reggie?" I asked.

"I don't know," Shayna said, her eyes firing darts at her sister.

"I don't know," Deborah said, her eyes catching the darts and returning them to Shayna's direction.

It wasn't just weird sisterly tension in the room. There was something else that was causing them to brawl.

Shayna glanced at me. "Why are you looking for him?"

"Good question," I said.

"Probably not because he wants to sleep with him again," Deborah said, with a nasty grin..

Shayna's cheeks flooded with color, and her entire face pinched in anger. "Shut up, Deborah."

"You slept with Reggie?" I asked, more surprised than amused.

"You aren't supposed to be talking to me," Shayna said, avoiding the question. "You can't even be near me."

"You sure like to be near Reggie, though, don't you, sis?" Deborah said, the grin on her face nastier now.

Shayna grimaced, pushed herself to her knees, and leapt at Deborah. Deborah, though, was ready and rolled away from her, kicking her feet at Shayna's hands. Shayna managed to get hold of an ankle, though, and held on. Deborah, in turn, reached over and grabbed a handful of Shayna's hair.

Something moved near the back of the room, and I glanced in that direction.

Bob the cat wandered out of the back room. He sat down, scratched an ear, then surveyed each of us. He was clearly unimpressed.

"You slept with Reggie while Benny was alive?" I asked Shayna.

"None of your damn beeswax, Deuce," Shayna said, trying to extract her hair from Deborah's hand.

"She's been sleeping with him for the last six months," Deborah yelled, shaking her ankle but unable to slip Shayna's grip.

"So have you!" Shayna yelled. She let go of Deborah's ankle for a moment and reached higher, sinking her nails into Deborah's thigh.

Deborah shrieked and pulled harder on Shayna's hair, stretching her neck into what looked to me like a very uncomfortable position.

As they struggled and grunted, I thought about Reggie Hamlin sleeping with both Deborah and Shayna. The first question was obviously, why? but from Reggie's perspective, I could see it. A kid in his twenties bedding one attractive older woman, much less two, was probably his version of winning the lottery. Why they would've been agreeable was another story, but it wasn't like either of them was the most virtuous of women. If they were going to sleep with anyone in the store, I would've thought it might have been the part-timer, Jake, given the description Reggie gave me. It was odd, though, that they'd both been involved with Benny's manager.

Between Reggie, Benny, and Odell, Land O' Rugs had been seeing some pretty weird stuff.

Bob strolled over next to me, gave me the once-over, evidently decided that I presented no threat to him, and sat down to watch the action.

They were at a stalemate, but neither would give in, and they continued grunting at each other, interrupted by small shrieks of pain.

I thought again about the three men that worked at the store, and a question worked its way into my head.

"Was Reggie involved in Killer Kids?" I asked. "With Odell and Benny?"

Deborah held tight to Shayna's hair, but Shayna's grip on Deborah's thigh weakened and she twitched in my direction, like I'd punched the right button.

"No," Shayna said, but her voice had zero conviction in it.

"Yes!" Deborah yelled, giving Shayna's hair a violent pull as she kicked out from under her grip and rolled away from her. She was in control now, on her knees, Shayna's hair in both hands and Shayna grabbing at those hands.

Deborah leveled her eyes at me. "The entire thing was Reggie's idea."

56

"I thought it was Odell's idea," I said, trying not reveal too much shock.

Deborah rolled her eyes. "Please. Odell's never had an idea in his entire life."

Now, that sounded exactly right.

"The entire thing was Reggie's idea," Deborah repeated, adjusting her grip on Shayna's hair. "He just wanted Odell's money."

"And Benny's, too, right?" I asked.

Deborah hesitated, as if there was an invisible line in the conversation and she wasn't sure whether to cross it. She blinked several times and glanced at her sister.

"And Benny's, too," Deborah finally said. "And Benny gave it to him. Didn't he, Shayna?"

Shayna remained silent, her hands wrapped around her sister's wrists.

"He did give it to him," Deborah said, shaking her head at her sister's silence. "But Shayna didn't want him to. Which was why Shayna stuck that knife in his chest and put him in your van."

Shayna started thrashing for all she was worth. "I did what? You shut the hell up, Deborah! I did not kill Benny!"

Deborah leaned back, trying to leverage her weight as she attempted to maintain control of Shayna's hair. "Oh, bull. Reggie told me how you did it and how you tossed Benny in Deuce's van because you knew how it would look." Deborah smirked. "You were so pissed at Benny for dumping your savings into Killer Kids, and you just couldn't take it anymore."

Shayna screamed, and Bob turned himself in a circle and sat back down to watch. Shayna moved like she'd been electrocuted, and Deborah couldn't hang on, Shayna's hair slipping out of her hands. Shayna rolled over, crouched like a jaguar about to pounce, and Deborah scooted away on her butt, fear washing over her face.

I'd been a bystander long enough. As Shayna jumped at Deborah, I caught her from behind and wrapped my arms around her.

She kicked and thrashed and threw her head back, trying to crack me in the face with her skull. But her head just kept bouncing off my chest.

"I didn't kill Benny! I didn't kill Benny!" Shayna screamed, kicking and trying to wriggle out of my arms. "I didn't kill Benny."

Deborah was still scooting away, but fear was now riding heavy in her expression, like I might let go of her raging sister at any moment.

After a few more seconds, Shayna's body sagged and she stopped kicking. Her body jerked several times, and I realized she was sobbing.

"I didn't kill Benny," she said, but it was no

longer a scream. It was a whine, full of pain and exhaustion and sadness. “I didn’t kill Benny.”

I eased my hold on her and her body continued to sag and I let her go to her knees. She brought her hands to her face.

“I didn’t kill Benny,” she repeated, her voice hoarse and worn and exhausted. “Reggie did.”

Bob the cat pawed at his ear, like he couldn’t believe what we were hearing.

57

"Reggie killed Benny?" I said, the words feeling funny coming off my tongue as I spoke them.

Shayna's limp figure managed a nod.

"That's absurd," Deborah said, but watching her sister carefully and making sure she was out of striking distance. "He told me you killed Benny."

Shayna lifted her head. Her tears had turned her mascara into smudgy black circles around her eyes. Her cheeks were flushed pink. She wiped at her eyes, streaking the mascara to the sides.

"Of course that's what he told you, Deborah," she croaked, saying "Deborah" much in the same way you'd expect someone to say "Disease-ridden whore." Her mouth tightened, grimaced, then worked its way into a bitter smile. "Reggie's been lying to you from day one." She shook her head. "To both of us."

Bob bumped his head against my leg. I reached over and scratched his ears. He pressed his head harder against my leg, and we both kept our eyes on Shayna.

She wiped harder at her eyes. "Killer Kids was

just a way for Reggie to steal money, all right? He was never serious about turning it into something real. He was just in it for the money."

"It was a scam?" I asked.

She nodded. "He was using Odell all along. He was just looking to take everyone's money."

Deborah squinted at her sister. "Why were you sleeping with him, then?"

"Same reason you were," she said, frowning at her sister. "Because he was good-looking and available."

"But you and Benny were married," I said.

Shayna looked at me like I was the Baby New Year. "Not everyone has your stupid fairy-tale-ass marriage, Deuce."

It was the first time I'd ever heard anyone describe my marriage like that. Did she really think it was a fairy tale? Julianne and I were happy and in love, but our marriage was work, just like anyone else's. It was strange to hear it described as if it was better than everyone else's.

"Benny and I should've gotten divorced years ago," Shayna said. "He cheated on me, and I cheated on him. We both knew. Our marriage was over a long time ago."

"Yeah, because he knew you still loved Deuce," Deborah said, a wicked smile slithering across her face.

Uh, whoa. Awkward.

Shayna cut her eyes to her sister. "Relationship analysis from the town slut. How ironic."

Deborah wrinkled her nose, then shrugged, like she'd heard it before and grown comfortable with her role in Rose Petal.

Shayna turned back to me. "So, yeah. I had an affair with Reggie. But I didn't know he was stealing Benny's money. Not at first, anyway."

Bob curled up in a ball next to me.

"How did you find out?" I asked.

"Benny," she said. "He figured it out. He found it on the computers, here at the store. He found the account number where they'd deposited the money. It was supposed to be some sort of savings account, but Reggie started acting funny. So Benny found the account and guess what?" Her face clouded over with disgust. "Money was gone."

"All of it?"

She nodded. "All of it. All that we had given him. All that Odell had given him. And all that Billy had given him."

"Billy?" I asked, surprised to hear his name. "Caldwell?"

"She's sleeping with him, too," Deborah chimed in.

Shayna ignored her. "Yes, Billy invested, too. And Reggie took it all."

"What did he do with it?"

"Hell if I know," Shayna said, rubbing her knees with her hands. "But it was gone."

Everything she was telling me made sense but seemed a little surreal. And I wasn't sure how I was supposed to determine whether Shayna was telling the truth.

"So why haven't you told anyone this?" I said. "If he killed Benny, why haven't you said anything? And why have you been content to let people think I did it?"

She pulled her eyes away from mine and studied her hands on her knees. "Because I'm stupid, Deuce."

I let that hang in the room until she was ready to continue.

"I let Billy lead me by the nose," she finally said. "Benny and I were a mess financially. That money he gave Reggie was, honest to God, all we had. When we found out that was gone, we knew we were screwed. That's why Benny confronted Reggie."

"He confronted him?"

"Same morning they found Benny in your van."

"So you knew Reggie killed him?" I asked.

"I had an idea," she said, still staring at her hands. "But I couldn't prove it. I called Billy as soon as the police called to tell me. I was crazy, drunk, out of my mind. And there was the possibility that *maybe* you could've killed him. It was Billy's idea to hit you with the lawsuit and to file the restraining order. Benny left me with nothing. Suing you was the only way to get my hands on any money."

"Idiot," Deborah whispered.

Shayna laughed. "Yeah, I'm the idiot. At least I didn't talk my friends into trying to kick Deuce out of his Room Daddy job because Reggie suggested it."

Deborah's face froze, all the collagen in her lips and cheeks coming to an abrupt halt.

"That true?" I asked, though I was already certain that it was.

Shayna raised an eyebrow and smiled at her sister, happy to have put her on the spot.

Deborah managed to thaw her expression and gave a slow nod. "Yes. I brought it up to Sharon Ann."

She blinked rapidly, replaying something in her mind. "And yes, it was Reggie's idea. Goddamn him."

Reggie seemed to have quite the power of manipulation.

"He said everyone would end up thanking me," she said. "Since everyone was saying you were the one that killed Benny, they'd thank me for helping to have you removed."

"But I thought you said he told you Shayna killed Benny?"

She continued blinking, letting it all play out in her head. "He did. After the meeting last night."

"Ask her why Benny ended up in your van," Shayna said, staring at her sister.

Deborah shifted, as if a sheet of tacks had been placed in her underwear. "What are you talking about?"

"What did you tell Reggie about me?" Shayna said, but there was very little question in her tone. "What did you tell him to try and get him to dump me? You just said it a minute ago."

Deborah thought, blinked some more, then cleared her throat. "I told him you still loved Deuce."

Seriously. Awkward.

Shayna nodded. "Exactly. You gave him the perfect person to put Benny's murder on."

Deborah looked at her sister. She swallowed hard, her lips pressed together, as the realization dawned on her that she had done just that.

Shayna shook her head, like it didn't surprise her. "Reggie's managed to get everyone looking everywhere but where they should be looking. At *him*."

As I tried to keep it all straight in my head, I had

to admit that it fit. Reggie had scammed them all several times over and played everyone against one another.

Bob stretched out next to my leg and pushed his head against me again. I looked down at the cat.

Reggie had played me, too.

58

Something fell in the back of the store, and Bob scrambled to his feet and took off for parts unknown.

Shayna and Deborah turned around, and I stood, thinking it was going to be Reggie.

Wrong.

Detective Willie Bell stumbled in, holding the side of his head with one hand and clutching something that looked like a gargantuan phone book in his other arm.

"Nobody move," he said, his hand pressed firmly to the side of his head. He wavered a bit and swayed to his left.

"Are you all right?" I asked.

He dropped the phone book, and it landed on his foot. He howled and sank to his butt.

"Oh," Shayna said. "Sample book."

"Sample book?" I said.

She nodded at the phone book. "Rug samples. A ton of 'em. I can't even pick that thing up."

"Are you all right?" I asked again.

He had one hand pressed to his head, the other wrapped tightly around his foot. "Don't move, I said."

He rocked on his rear end. He finally took the hand away from his temple, revealing a red welt the size of a tennis ball.

"What happened?" I asked.

"It hit me in the head," he said, wincing, still rocking.

"Just reached out and took a swing?"

Both Deborah and Shayna laughed. Detective Willie Bell did not.

"It fell off the shelf." He winced and tried to focus. "I'm here to arrest you, Deuce Winters." He let go of the foot, tried to stand on it, and fell over to the side, reeling in pain. "Dammit! I think it's broken."

"A shame," I said.

He pointed a finger at me, then lost his balance and rolled again. "Don't move. You're in violation of that restraining order."

I looked at Shayna.

"He ain't doin' nothin', Willie," she said, frowning at him. "It's fine."

He looked at the two sisters, took in their appearance. "You two all right? You look like you were attacked." He nodded at me. "He do that to you?"

"Oh, Willie. Shut up," Deborah said, dismissing him with a wave.

Willie's face reddened.

I took several steps toward the fallen detective and extended my hand. "Can I help you up?"

He kept his eyes away from me for a moment, then finally looked up at me. "I'm still gonna get you, you know that?"

"No, you aren't, Detective."

He squinted again, probably thinking it made him look tough. "Oh, I always get my man, Winters. Always. You know why?" A smug smile settled on his face. "Because I'm a details guy. That's why I'm here right now."

"You're here because you're a details guy?"

"Yep," he said, giving a curt nod. "I followed you over here. Then I saw Miss Shayna in here, and I knew you were up to no good."

"Up to no good?" I said. "Seriously? Of all the clichés you could use, that's the one you're gonna go with?"

His cheeks darkened again in embarrassment.

I retracted my hand. "You know what? Sit there on your butt, then. These ladies can tell you what they just told me. Maybe that'll help you get your man." I headed for the door.

"Hey! Wait!" he yelled, crawling on the floor, his damaged foot dragging behind him. "Stop right there!"

I didn't.

Shayna reached out and pushed him, and he fell onto his side with a thud.

"Shut up and sit still, Willie," she said. "We've got something to tell you."

59

I pushed open the door and stepped out into the sticky, humid afternoon air, irritated, angry, and wondering exactly how heavy that swatch catalog was. As I headed for the minivan, I noticed a car coming into the lot. Not just any old car, though.

Odell Barnabas's truck/station wagon.

He pulled up in front of me, leaned across the passenger seat, and through the open window said, "Hey, Ace."

"Hey, Odell."

"Get in," he said.

"No thanks. My car's right there."

Plus, I didn't have time to self-administer a tetanus shot before jumping in.

"Come on," he said, waving me in. "I wanna show you something. It'll only take a minute."

Isn't that what the pedophiles say?

The thing was, Odell Barnabas was next on my list of people to talk to. Based on what both Shayna and Deborah just told me, I wanted to find out from him exactly what he thought of Reggie. Not that I expected anything substantial, but I wanted to cover all the bases before I talked to Victor again.

I opened the door, and it creaked as it swung open. He waved a hand across the seat, knocking several Styrofoam cups and a newspaper to the floor. Against my better judgment, I sat down and closed the door.

He pulled the wagon out of the lot and turned right. His hands were tight on the wheel, and he looked much more tense than when I'd seen him before.

"What's going on, Odell?" I asked. "You look kinda funny."

As soon as it came out of my mouth, I hoped he wouldn't take that the wrong way. Or right way. Or whatever.

But if it hit too close to home, he didn't react to it. In fact, he kept his eyes straight ahead and his fingers clamped to the wheel.

"Odell?" I asked. "Where are we going?"

"You'll find out when we get there," a voice said from behind me.

I twisted in the seat.

Buried under mounds of old clothing, fast-food bags, and other assorted things that belonged in a garbage can was Reggie Hamlin, pointing a gun at me.

60

We drove north out of Rose Petal, around the lake.

"So," I said. "You guys working together now?"

"No talking," Reggie said from his covert spot in the trash.

I glanced at Odell. He was tight-lipped, his jaw set. And either a gnat buzzed his nose or he gave me a barely noticeable shake of his head.

As a kid, I was always a daydreamer. Drifting off, thinking about playing in the NFL, saving some beautiful girl, or fronting a band in front of a hundred thousand people was not an unusual way for me to spend an afternoon. But in all those years of thinking about totally ridiculous, far-out situations, never did I ever think I'd find myself riding next to a guy with the worst toupee I'd ever seen, held captive by a college kid beneath a pile of garbage.

Maybe I just hadn't been very imaginative.

Reggie didn't want any talking, but I assumed he'd already instructed Odell where to go, as he seemed to know where he was heading without any word from our captor.

I admit, I was a little nervous. I'd never had a gun pointed at me before, and I was being held against my will. But there was this buzz in my brain that kept telling me this seemed more like a cartoon gone bad than something that was putting my life in jeopardy. Ignorance can sometimes be its own reward.

We circled around the side of the lake into an unincorporated part of the county. The landscape was patchy. Overgrown lots, forty-year-old ranch homes, roadside stores that had either seen better days or had always been wishing for them. Every few years some developer made noise about dropping a bunch of homes in the area, but the lack of infrastructure and roads running out to the highway would eventually be too much to overcome. As a result, the north end of the lake had become a mishmash of a community. College students, drug dealers, loners, and a bunch of other folks who didn't want to be classified as anything.

It was exactly the kind of place I *didn't* want to be with Odell and Reggie and a gun.

Odell turned the station wagon onto a dirt road, and we bumped and hopped our way about a quarter of a mile, until the tires crunched to a stop.

A dilapidated trailer home sat among several humongous oak trees. The trailer was actually at an angle, the left side lifted up on several sets of cinder blocks, the right side resting on the dirt. A door hung loosely in the center of it, a giant pink smiley face painted on it. It looked deserted.

"This is my place," Odell said.

"You live here?" I asked.

"Couple years now." He shrugged. "No air-conditioning, so it gets hot, but other than that, it works out pretty good."

There was absolutely not a single detail about Odell's home that looked pretty good.

"I'm gettin' out the back," Reggie said, rustling around in the back. "You both stay put until I come around to the front."

I heard him scoot backward, open the gate, and step out.

"He thinks I got more money here, Ace," Odell whispered.

"Do you?"

"Not a penny, Ace. And he's gonna be mad as a hungry rooster when I tell him."

From bad to worse.

I caught a glimpse of Reggie coming up along my side of the car in the passenger-side mirror. "Don't say anything, then."

"Ace, he's gonna . . ."

"Just keep pretending, Odell."

"I don't get why he's doin' this," Odell said. "If he needs money, I coulda lended it to him."

Reggie tapped on the window with the gun and motioned for me to get out. I did, and he used the gun to guide me to the front of the car.

"Now you, Odell," Reggie said, his eyes on me. It was clear that he viewed me as a bigger threat than Odell. Smart guy, Reggie.

Odell got out of the driver's side and joined me at the front of the car, patting down his pompadour.

"What'd Shayna and Deborah tell you?" Reggie asked.

"Nothing," I said.

Reggie smiled. "Please. Those two couldn't keep their mouths shut for a million dollars."

I didn't say anything.

"I'm gonna guess they told you a little too much," he said.

"You could tell me it's not true," I said.

"And you wouldn't believe me."

"Probably not."

He kept the gun pointed at my chest. "So let's not do that."

"What are you two talking about?" Odell asked, his face screwed up in puzzlement.

Reggie stayed silent.

"Reggie killed Benny, Odell," I said. "And he stole your money. Benny's and Billy's, too."

Odell stared at me for a long moment, attempting to absorb my words. The expression on his face, though, made me wonder if I'd accidentally spoken in a foreign language, because he was looking at me like he hadn't understood a word I said.

"Killer Kids was a sham," I said.

Odell blinked. He moved his glance to Reggie. "You took my money, Reg?"

Reggie stayed silent.

"And you killed Benny?" Odell said, pressing, his tone uncomprehending.

Reggie's mouth twitched, but he kept it closed.

"And you weren't serious about Killer Kids?" Odell said, a bit louder now. Then he shook his head, like a four-year-old who was putting his foot down. "No way. I don't believe that. No way."

"Believe it, Odell," I said. "And if I'm guessing right, he's the one that clubbed me on the back of the head at the school, too."

"You two can shut up right about now," Reggie said, moving the gun from me to Odell and back to me. "Odell, where's the money?"

"Killer Kids is gonna be awesome," Odell continued, as if he was pleading to an investor that could make his dream a reality. "One of a kind. I mean, other than Tough Tykes. Why wouldn't you believe that?"

"Shut up, Odell," Reggie said.

The fact that Reggie hadn't bothered to deny anything so far indicated to me that what Shayna and Deborah told me was indeed true. Reggie was the igniter of the flames that had burned through my life the previous few days. But I still wasn't sure why.

"I won't shut up," Odell said, taking several steps past me, now closer to Reggie than I was and apparently unafraid of the gun Reggie was holding. "Killer Kids will work! And I want my damn money back!" He edged closer to Reggie.

Odell's lack of fear caught Reggie by surprise, and he appeared uncertain how to handle it. He centered the gun on Odell but took a step backward.

"Why'd you take the money, Reggie?" I asked. "You gave me that whole song and dance about having to work at the store because of your father and school."

Reggie's eyes were pinballing between Odell and me. "I'm sick of working, and I'm sick of school, man. But if I quit either one, my dad would cut me loose. And those two broads were getting to be too much for me. I gotta get the hell outta this dumb-ass town, anyway."

"So you just decided to steal?" I said.

Odell was inching toward Reggie, and Reggie

was inching backward, as if the gun he was holding was just a water pistol.

"Benny should've minded his own business," Reggie said. "Should've stayed off the computer and out of my stuff."

A breeze blew in, rustling the old oaks. Normally, I wouldn't have heard that. But with the three of us standing there, alone and isolated, the movement in the trees was as loud as someone banging a drum in my ear.

"I want my damn money," Odell reiterated.

Reggie's eyes—and the gun—were locked firmly on Odell. I wanted to tell Odell to relax, but I knew that having Reggie's attention focused elsewhere could be an advantage for me.

"You lied about Bob," I said, just to keep him talking.

Reggie's eyes narrowed. "I what?"

"You lied about Bob."

Odell turned his head a fraction in my direction. "What about Bob? Is he all right?"

"You and that stupid cat," Reggie muttered, more annoyed than amused.

Bob was, in fact, the one that truly confirmed to me that Reggie was behind everything. As he'd strolled over and lain down next to me during Shayna and Deborah's wrestling match, something occurred to me. The first time I met Reggie, he told me that Bob didn't go near anyone and that he'd freaked out when Odell attempted to catnap him. That led me to think two things. Bob was an okay cat, and Odell had been fired for another reason.

"You didn't try and steal Bob, did you, Odell?" I asked.

Odell's shoulders twitched. "Uh, actually, yeah. I did."

I still had some things to learn about being an investigator.

"Reggie hates that cat, Ace," Odell said. "Couldn't stand to see him get treated like that. So I wanted to take him home." He refocused on Reggie. "I thought you woulda been happy that I wanted Bob. I couldn't believe you fired me."

"I was just looking for a reason, you moron," Reggie said, sneering at him. "I wanted your ass outta there, and you trying to take that damn cat with you gave me all I needed to can your dumb butt."

So I'd gotten it half right. He wanted Odell gone so he'd be out of the way and unable to check the computer, like Benny had.

"Odell, I'm not kidding," Reggie said, lifting the gun a little higher, reemphasizing that he was holding a gun. "Give me your money or I'll shoot you."

"I ain't got nothin' to give you, Reg," Odell said, inching forward again. "And I want what you took back." Odell took another step. "Killer Kids is gonna happen!"

"Odell," I said. "Relax."

But I could see he'd already made up his mind. Gun or no gun, he was going after Reggie Hamlin.

He charged, and I was right behind him, trying to grab him and keep him from getting shot.

But Odell was quicker than I ever would've given him credit for. He was out of my reach and on top of Reggie before I could get my hands on him.

Reggie was either too surprised or too afraid to fire the gun. Odell crashed into him, grabbing onto the hand Reggie was holding the gun with. They did kind of an awkward dance, spun in a circle, the gun pointed straight up in the air, and then collapsed to the ground.

I was locked in on the gun as I sprinted toward them. Reggie hadn't fired it, but I knew it was more likely to go off now that things had gone downhill. All I wanted to do was take that thing out of commission and make sure it couldn't hurt anyone, a move that would take a desperate act on my part.

As I dove on top of them and entered the fray, I grabbed the one thing I could think of that might do the job.

I ripped Odell's toupee from his head and smothered the gun with it.

61

Reggie was no match for the two of us.

Odell was punching at his face, I had the gun pinned under the pompadour, and we were both on top of him, several hundreds pounds that were making it tough for Reggie to breathe.

His fingers loosened on the gun, and I pulled it out of his hands with the toupee. Reggie immediately brought a hand up to his face to defend against Odell's punches. I rolled off the pile.

I'd never held a gun before. I was very un-Texan in that regard. They scared the heck out of me, and I wasn't looking to change that.

I pushed to my knees, wrapped the gun up in Odell's hair, and heaved it as far away from us as I could.

"Nice throw," a voice said from behind us.

I twisted around.

Victor was standing there with Detective Willie Bell.

"About time," I said.

Victor looked at me, then at Odell pummeling a

now lifeless Reggie. "Seems like things are under control."

Bell moved over and pulled Odell off Reggie, whose nose was now bleeding from both nostrils.

"Those two chicks at the rug store filled us in," Victor said. "They saw you get in Odell's car, so we thought we'd come out here and make sure you guys were okay. Came in the back way so no one would shoot us."

"I thought you were with Jillian."

Victor shook his head. "I dropped her off. I knew you were heading to the rug store. I could tell when I left you."

I pointed at Bell. "So he's not here to arrest me?"

"Nope."

Bell pulled Reggie to his feet, slapped the cuffs on him, and gave a satisfied nod. "Just happy to have this all taken care of." He marched off, Reggie Hamlin in tow.

I'd roll my eyes at him another time.

I got up and dusted myself off.

Odell sat up. He was as bald as Victor, and seeing him without the toupee was just creepy. As strange as the rug was, I'd grown accustomed to seeing it on his head, and his appearance changed dramatically without it.

He touched the corner of his mouth, then looked at me. "He really take all that money, Ace?"

I nodded. "I think so, Odell."

"Think I'll get it back?"

"I have no idea."

He gave a slow nod. "Think I could have Bob now?"

I couldn't help but smile. "I'm not sure, but I'll bet that's a possibility."

"Where's the gun, Ace? And my hair?"

There was no embarrassment in the question, and I liked him immensely more for it.

"It's over there," I said, pointing. "By your trailer."

"We'll probably need that gun," Victor said.

Odell stood and trudged over to the crooked trailer. He picked up the toupee and walked back to me. He unspooled the pompadour and handed me the gun.

"Sorry I threw it," I said. I motioned to the hair. "Your . . . that."

"It's okay, Ace," he said, looking sad. "I've got another one."

Victor joined us, and I handed him the gun. I figured he had a better idea of what to do with it than what I did.

"I ask you a question, Ace?" Odell said, rolling the toupee over in his hands.

"Sure."

He squinted into the sunshine. "You think Killer Kids was a stupid idea?"

Guns and kids was about as stupid of an idea as I'd ever run across. But there was something about Odell's earnestness, his sadness at the idea that his idea might've been fruitless from the get-go that prevented me from telling him that.

"No," I said to Odell. "I think you had a good idea."

Victor turned away, presumably to hide whatever bemused expression was gracing his mug.

Odell's face brightened, and he stood a little

taller, his entire mood buoyed by my statement. "I thought so, Ace. I thought so."

He headed toward the front door of his crooked trailer, the one with the pink smiley face on it, then turned around when he got there. "And you know what?"

"What's that, Odell?"

"When I open Killer Kids, I'm gonna give you a free membership," he said, nodding. "Make you a charter member."

"That'd be nice."

He raised an eyebrow. "Of course, you're still free to buy in, Ace, if you can come up with the dough." He tapped his temple. "I'll figure it out. You can count on it."

I did not doubt him.

62

Team Turkey was in last place.

It was a week later, and Julianne and I were standing off to the side of the expansive green field, watching the preschool Olympics. Team Turkey was having trouble in the Duck, Duck, Goose event, the hopscotch event, and the fifteen-yard dashes. It appeared that Carly's class had not put in much training time.

But all that really mattered was that their shirts were by far the coolest out there.

All in all, things were back to normal for me in Rose Petal.

"Sharon Ann wouldn't even say hello to me," Julianne said, a sly grin beneath her sunglasses. "I waved at her, and she pretended not to see me."

"Maybe she didn't see you."

"I was maybe four feet from her."

"Oh."

The normalcy included Sharon Ann acting like nothing had ever happened and Deborah keeping a good distance away from me. It irritated me that

Deborah had used her friendship with Sharon Ann to attempt to railroad me out of my Room Dad job, but in the end, there'd been no harm done.

Julianne let out an ear-piercing whistle as Carly took her turn in the fifteen-yard dash. Carly's arms and legs flailed as she made her way toward the finish line.

"Shayna's lawsuit was officially dismissed this morning," Julianne said as she clapped for our daughter. "And the TRO was withdrawn yesterday."

I hadn't seen Billy or Shayna since I'd seen Shayna at Land O' Rugs, and I hoped it would stay that way. I didn't need either of them in my life.

"I'd imagine Billy is eyeing that Hamlin kid's dad now," she continued. "If he owns that rug store, he may have some assets that might be of interest in a wrongful death suit."

Reggie Hamlin had pled not guilty to Benny Barnes's murder at his arraignment. The judge had denied bail, so he was spending his days and nights behind bars.

"Lovely," I said, shading my eyes from the sun. "I truly could not care less."

"And did I hear that voice mail right?" Julianne asked, peering over her glasses at me. "From Victor?"

I laughed. "Yes, you did."

Victor wanted to employ me. He said I'd done a good enough job as an investigator and he wanted to bring me on as a part-time contractor.

"I told him I'd think about it."

"You what?"

"I told him I'd think about it," I repeated, watching Carly roll around on the grass with one of her friends, her laugh drifting across the field. "After the summer camp deal."

I'd called Jimmy Landry and told him we were on for the football camps. He'd already sent me a bunch of paperwork I had to look over, and we were working on a schedule. Most importantly, when he'd offered free swim lessons for Carly as part of the deal, Julianne gave her approval.

"Yeah, well, I'm not so sure I like that one," Julianne said, turning back to the field.

"Let's worry about it when it's time to worry about it."

In truth, I wasn't sure I wanted to work as a part-time investigator. But I was intrigued by the idea. Maybe I was getting a little bored at home or maybe I was just looking for something to keep me occupied while I was at school or maybe I was just flattered that Victor asked. I wasn't looking to jump into it, but it was kind of fun to think about.

So things were back to normal.

"You've had a rough couple of weeks," Julianne said, slipping her arm around my waist.

"Nothing that left any permanent damage."

"I know, but still. So I thought you needed a gift."

"A gift?"

Carly ambled over to us, her ponytail falling out of the rubber band and her cheeks flushed bright pink.

"Did you guys see me run?" she asked, out of breath.

"We did," I said. "You were awesome."

"I know," she said, nodding, as if her awesomeness just came so easily to her. She looked at Julianne. "How come you aren't at work, Mama?"

"Because I came to watch you," Julianne said. "That okay?"

"Sure, yeah," she said, raising her little eyebrows. "Okay, I have to go now." She pivoted and ran back to her Team Turkey teammates.

"She's hilarious," Julianne said.

"She is." I put my arm around my wife's shoulders. "So. You were talking about a gift. For me."

"I was," she said. "Bet you can't guess what it is."

"Trip to Bermuda?"

"Wrong."

"Season tickets to the Cowboys?"

"Wrong."

"My own pet llama?"

"Close." She squeezed her arm around my waist. "How about another kid?"

Whoa. "Another kid?"

"Yeah."

"So you wanna go home right now and get the process started?" I asked. "Like we did the other day?"

She pulled the sunglasses from her face and looked up at me. "Let's not even go home. Just drop right here and get started."

Excitement percolated inside me. "Really?"

She laughed. "No, not right this second. But I'm ready. She needs a little sister or brother. And you need more kids to shepherd. We both do." Her smile softened. "I'm just ready."

We'd always planned on having at least two kids, maybe three. We wanted a few years in between each so that we could enjoy the different stages of each child without stealing from the others. But I hadn't given much thought to whether we were at that point yet. I was still enjoying Carly, and it seemed like just yesterday we were bringing her home from the hospital.

"Cowboys tickets would be cheaper," I said.

She arched an eyebrow at me. "True. But Cowboys tickets don't enable you to have your way with me when we start trying to make a baby. Like tonight."

"Excellent point," I said, smiling at her.

She returned my smile, and my eyes drifted toward the field. I liked that she was ready. I liked that she wanted more. And I liked that she wanted another child with me.

But was I ready for Baby Number Two?

I was watching the kids out on the field but was seeing dirty diapers, long nights, and crying jags. The crying jags were mine.

"So. What do you think?" she asked, leaning against me.

I was thinking a lot of things, but one thing in particular.

So much for normal.

Keep reading for a special sneak preview
of the next Deuce Winters mystery,
available in October 2012!

1

"The King of Soccer is missing," Julianne said into my ear.

I was standing on the sideline, sweating, concentrating on the swarm of tiny girls chasing after a soccer ball. As the head coach of my daughter's soccer team, The Mighty, Fightin', Tiny Mermaids, it was my sworn duty to scream myself silly on Saturday afternoons, hoping they might play a little soccer rather than chase butterflies and roll around in the grass. As usual, I was failing.

I gave my wife a quick glance. "What?"

"The King of Soccer is missing," she repeated.

Before I could respond, Carly sprinted toward me from the center of the field, ponytails and tiny cleats flying all around her.

"Daddy," she said, huffing and puffing. "How am I doing?"

I held my hand out for a high five. "Awesome, dude."

She nodded as if she already knew. "Good. Hey, are we almost done?"

"About ten more minutes."

She thought about that for a moment, shrugged, and said, "Oh. Okay." Then she turned and sprinted back to the mass of girls surrounding the ball.

Except for the ones holding hands and skipping around the mass of girls surrounding the ball.

I took a deep breath, swallowed the urge to yell something soccer-ish, and turned back to Julianne. "What?"

She was attempting to smother a smile and failing. "Sorry. Didn't meant to interrupt the strategy session, Coach."

"Whatever."

She put her hand on my arm. "I was trying to warn you. MoisesCarles is missing."

MoisesCarles, aka The King of Soccer, was the president of the Rose Petal Youth Soccer Association. He oversaw approximately two hundred teams, close to two thousand kids, five hundred volunteers, and about a billion obnoxious parents.

He was also a bit of a jerk.

"Missing?"

"Hasn't been seen in three days, and Belinda wants to talk to you about it."

I shifted my attention back to the game. Carly broke free from the pack with the ball and loped toward the open goal. My heart jumped, and I moved down the sideline with her. "Go! Keep going!"

Several of the girls trailed behind her, laughing and giggling, not terribly concerned that they were about to be scored upon.

Carly approached the goal, settled the ball in

front of herself, shuffled her feet, and took a mighty swing at the ball.

It glanced off the side of her foot and rolled wide of the goal and over the touchline.

My heart sank, and the gaggle of parents behind me in the bleachers groaned.

Carly turned in my direction, grinned, and gave me a thumbs-up. I smiled back at her through the pain and returned the thumbs-up.

She sprinted back toward her teammates.

Maybe we needed to practice a little more.

I walked back up the sideline to Julianne. "Why does she want to talk to me about it?"

"I think it has to do with you being a superb private eye and all," Julianne said.

"I'm not a private eye."

"Those fancy cards you and Victor hand out beg to differ, Coach."

After successfully proving my innocence in the murder of an old high school rival, I'd reluctantly joined forces with Victor Anthony Doolittle in his investigation business. On a very, very, very limited basis. We were still trying to figure out if we could coexist, and the jury was still deliberating.

I frowned. "What does *missing* mean? Like he's not here today?"

Julianne shrugged. "Dunno. But you can ask her yourself." She tilted her chin in the direction of the sideline. "She's coming your way, Coach." She kissed me on the cheek. "And don't forget. We have a date tonight."

"A date?" I asked.

"Well, a date sounds classier than using you for

sex," she said, slipping her sunglasses over her eyes. "But call it what you like. Coach." She gave a small wave and walked away.

I started to say something about being objectified—and how I was in favor of it—but Belinda Stansfield's gargantuan body ate up the space Julianne had just vacated.

"Deuce," Belinda said in between huffs and puffs. "Need your help."

Her crimson cheeks were drenched in sweat, and her gray T-shirt was ringed with perspiration. Actually, it appeared as if all 350 pounds of Belinda were ringed in perspiration.

She ran a meaty hand over her wet forehead and smoothed her coarse brown hair away from her face. She took another huff—or maybe it was a puff—and set her hands on her expansive hips.

"Middle of a game here, Belinda," I said, moving my gaze back to the field, which I found far more pleasant. "Can't it wait?"

"No can do, Deuce," she said. "This is serious business."

Carly tackled one of the opposing girls, literally threw her arms around her and took her to the grass. They dissolved into a pile of laughter as the ball squirted by them.

"Um, so is this, Belinda."

"Oh, please, honey," she said, shading her eyes from the sun. "These little girls care more about what's in the cooler after the game than the score. And these parents don't know a goal from a goose. You are a babysitter with a whistle. Get over yourself."

Couldn't have put it better myself.

"What's up?" I asked.

"Mo's done and gone and disappeared."

"Like, from the fields?"

"Like, from Rose Petal?"

Tara Little started crying and ran past me to her parents. We were now down a Fightin' Mermaid.

"Since when?"

"Today's Saturday," she said, swiping again at the sweat covering her face. "Last anyone saw him was Wednesday."

"Maybe he went on vacation," I said.

"Nope."

"Maybe he's taking a long nap."

"Deuce. I am not kidding."

The pimple-faced referee blew his whistle, and the girls ran faster than they'd run the entire game. They sprinted past me to the bleachers, where a cooler full of drinks and something made entirely of sugar awaited them. Serious soccer players, these little girls.

I took a deep breath, tired from yelling and baking in the sun, adjusted the visor on my head. "Okay. So he's missing."

She nodded, oceans of sweat cascading down her chubby face. "And there's something else you should know."

I watched the girls, red-faced and exhausted, sitting next to each other on the metal bleachers, sucking down juice boxes, munching on cookies, and swinging their legs back and forth.

There were worse ways to spend a Saturday.

"What's that?" I asked.

"Seventy-three thousand bucks," Belinda said.

"What? What are you talking about?"

She shifted her enormous body from one tree stump of a leg to the other.

"Mo's missing," Belinda said. "And he took seventy-three thousand dollars with him."

2

“All of the summer and fall registration fees,” Belinda said. “Gone.”

The girls were now chasing one another, the parents were chatting, and Belinda and I were sitting on the bottom of the bleachers.

“How is that possible?” I asked. “He just walked away with that much in cash?”

“The bank accounts are empty,” she said. “They were full on Tuesday. Before he disappeared.”

“Could be a coincidence.”

“And I could bc a ballcrina,” shc said, raising an eyebrow. “It ain’t a coincidence, Deuce.”

No, it probably wasn’t a coincidence. She was right about that.

“Don’t you guys have some sort of control in place for that kind of thing?” I asked. “I mean, with the accounts. Multiple signatures or something like that?”

She shook her head. “Nope. Last year, when Mo was reelected, he demanded full oversight. The board didn’t like it, but he said he’d walk without it. So they gave it to him.”

"Why did he want it?"

"No clue."

I spied Carly attaching herself to Julianne's leg. She was crying. Carly, not Julianne. Crying had become common after soccer games, the result of too much sugar and some physical exertion. It was less about being upset with something and more about it being time just to get on home.

"I want to hire you, Deuce," she said. "We want to hire you. The board. To find him and the money. You and that little dwarf, or whatever he is."

A smile formed on my lips. I wished Victor was there to hear her description of him.

"I'll need to talk to Victor," I told her. "The little dwarf. To make sure he's okay with it."

"You two got so much work you're turning away business?"

As a matter of fact, we did. Or rather, Victor did. Since our initial escapade, people had been seeking us out left and right. My agreement with Victor allowed me the flexibility to work only when I wanted to. Fortunately, he'd been more than capable of handling most of the work and I'd been left alone to play Mr. Mom to Carly.

"No," I said, attempting to be diplomatic. "But we don't take anything on unless both of us agree."

She thought about that for a moment, then nodded.

Then her stomach growled.

"There's one other thing," she said.

"What's that?"

"We can't pay you."

I pinched the bridge of my nose. "That's gonna be

a problem, Belinda. The little dwarf likes money. He tends to not work without it."

"I mean, we can't pay you up front," she clarified. "Everything we got, he took. You find him and the money, we'll pay you whatever we owe you."

I knew Victor was going to have a coronary over that.

"I'll talk to Victor and see what I can do," I said, standing.

She pushed her girth up off the bleachers, wobbled for a minute, then steadied herself. She wiped a massive hand across her wet brow.

"Well, I hope you can do something, Deuce," she said, a sour expression settling on her face. "Because that money? That's all we got. It doesn't come back, soccer don't come back."

"Really?"

"We are totally fee driven. Nothing in reserve. So unless you wanna foot the bill for uniforms and trophies and field space and insurance, and who the heck knows what else, we need that money."

I glanced over at the remaining girls. Carly had detached herself from Julianne and was now playing some bastardized version of tag. They weren't good at soccer, but I regularly espoused the virtues of team sports at a young age. They weren't winning games, but I believed they were getting something out of playing.

"Why would he take the money, Belinda?" I asked.

"I got no idea," she said, shaking her head. "I really don't, Deuce. But we gotta have the money back. Now him?" She waved a hand in the air. "I couldn't care less whether that weasel comes back."

"Weasel?"

Her eyes narrowed. "You don't know him all that well, do you?"

I shrugged. I knew him from around town and from soccer meetings. A little pompous, but other than that, I didn't think much at all about him.

"No," I admitted. "I guess not."

"Weasel," she said. "Pure weasel."

"Why's that?"

"Because that's the way the good Lord made him," she said, frowning. "Or Satan. Whichever."

"So you aren't surprised he took the money, then?" I asked.

"I'm a little surprised," she said. "Because I didn't think even he'd pull something like this. But you know what's more surprising?"

I looked past her. Julianne now had Carly in her arms and was waving at me. I was ready to go home and be objectified.

"Uh, no. What's more surprising?"

She hiked up her ill-fitting shorts and looked me dead in the eye.

"That no one's killed that weasel yet."